TWO

TWO

LAURENCE M. JANIFER

WILDSIDE PRESS

*This one is for
the timpanist*

TWO

For more information about this or other Wildside Press
books, please contact:

Wildside Press
P.O. Box 301
Holicong, PA 18928-0301
www.wildsidepress.com

First Wildside Printing: April 2003

ONE

"Marriage" (I said to this starved-looking woman, with eyes as big as a homeless orphan's—an orphan crazed on one of the jumpier addictives—whose name I hadn't caught) "is an honorable estate, instituted of God."

"But it's so strange," she said. She took a small, refined gulp at her champagne. "Marriage. I mean, after all—marriage. Not at all the expected sort of thing, is it? The less so, for a Survivor."

"Marriage is anti-survival?" I said, and took a gentler sip of my own.

"It's just that—well, you'll be away such a great deal, won't you? Your assignments—they run to a year each time, isn't that the way it goes?"

"That's the way it goes," I said. "But I've been picking and choosing my own for the last little while—and now I may not choose any at all."

"My goodness," she said. "And how will you—ah—survive, then?"

I shrugged and took another sip. She emptied her goblet, and looked at it wistfully. "Something will turn up," I said. "It usually does. By the way, what *is* your name?"

She gave me a smile so dreamy and distant I knew she was in a place all her own, and hardly at all in the Grand Ballroom the rest of us had come to inhabit. "Astarte," she said. "Astarte Finch."

"Nice to meet you," I said, looking around for rescue.

"Of course," Astarte Finch said, "it is rather traditional. I understand that many people *do* become married—not in our set, to be sure, but 'round Earth somewhere."

"On some worlds," I said, "nearly everybody does. Like most things, it varies." Where Mirella had got to, I couldn't imagine.

"I'm sure," Ms. Finch said vaguely. "It must add a touch of—well, of excitement to their—"

And somebody from Colonization bustled up and grabbed my arm. I had never before been glad to greet somebody from Colonization, but, as I'd been saying, things vary.

"Knave," he said—he was a tall, remarkably thin fellow with bright red hair and a pointed nose—"I've got to talk to you."

Astarte Finch stared at the new arrival as if he'd been a small slug crawling on a salad fork. I gave her a smile, and was careful not to make it a grin.

"Very sorry," I said, "but duty calls. You remember duty— stern daughter of the voice of God, or something."

"I'm sure," she said again, and looked down at her empty glass. She wandered off, probably to refill the thing six or eight times, and I turned the smile on the Colonization sahib.

"You don't have to talk to me," I said. "Your little green badge means nothing to me now. I am on leave. Indefinite damn leave. When I get over being on leave, I will notify you, the very first thing. It's the least I can do, and thank you. But—"

"You don't understand," he said, and what the Hell, maybe I didn't. "She's missing."

For one blank second I thought he meant Mirella. "What do you mean, missing?" I said. "She's off talking to somebody or other. It's a crowded room. You just—"

"She never appeared," he said. "That's not at all like her. There has been no notice. Note, tape, message—nothing. She can't be reached at the Palace, and there have been no sightings. Knave, I tell you—"

I sighed. "One small thing," I said. "Who the Hell are we talking about? And just for curiosity's sake, who the Hell are you?"

"Amy-Robsart," he said. "Amy-Robsart Berringer, for God's sake, who did you think I meant? I tell you, she's not here."

"And you are?"

"Deke. Claude Deke. What difference does it make? Knave, this is becoming an emergency."

"Well," I said, "when it gets to be one, let me know. But just because the youngest and quietest daughter of the Emperor decides to pass up one small dinner party, for one Survivor on leave, I don't really think—"

"I tell you, it's not like her," he said.

I sighed. "All right," I said. "It's not. She might not be one hundred per cent predictable—I've never met anybody who was. And even if something's happened—something emergency-like—what the Hell do you want *me* for?"

He sighed. "FoFeality," he said. "You understand." And, oddly enough, I did.

"You're afraid to let him loose on the situation," I said.

"Horace FoFeality," he said flatly. "It will be spread over the 3V in ninety minutes, over the newstapes in four hours. And that—I tell you in confidence, Knave—is all that will happen. For God's sake, Knave."

It wasn't all that confidential a fact: Horace FoFeality had a reputation that was one step short of public, and sixty or seventy short of acceptable.

I disengaged my arm. Gently. "Look," I said. "You're overreacting. It's been—what? An hour and a half since the dinner broke up. Nobody expected Amy-Robsart Berringer to turn up for the dinner itself, given the quality of official dinners. So she'd come in afterward, and greet some people politely, and shake hands, and show off whatever new outfit needed showing off, and go away again. Maybe."

"But—"

"And maybe she just got tired of the drill, for one evening. It happens, even to the quiet ones. I understand why you don't want FoFeality to take charge—but that's the Emperor's fault, and he should have known better; Palace Security Chief is not a political kind of job. He really should have known better."

"But you've got to find her," he said.

"I do not," I said. "She doesn't have to be found. She'll find herself, tonight or some time tomorrow, and she'll have a fairly good story to cover her vanishment, and it'll all blow the Hell over. Let it."

"You won't help?" he said. "This is an official request, Knave. From the household of the Emperor."

"I have been requested by any number of human beings, a variety of other people—Berigot, Gielli, Plenc, Tocks—and now and then by a printed invitation. I have never before been requested by an entire household, and I think—"

"Requested what? Where?" Mirella said, and I turned around.

"To do a job that doesn't need doing," I said.

She wrinkled her features. For a very cheerful face, Mirella's can look remarkably awful, when she has a point to make. The stage, or the 3V, lost a very showy overactor when she went into police work.

"They can't hook you in now," she said. "Indefinite leave, a nice testimonial dinner, a little plaque something or other. The plaque makes it official. You do not work here any more. Anyhow for a while."

"So I've been saying," I told her. "I suppose we can't actually sneak away yet, but—"

"Ms. Puffer," Claude Deke said, "perhaps I can make you understand the importance—"

"Mrs.," Mirella said. "Mrs. Mirella Knave, okay? There are people *like* Ms., I know there are, and fine, let them like it. Me, I had thirty years with it, and it is time for a change."

He smiled at her. It wasn't much of a smile, but he tried. "Mrs. Knave, then," he said. "I haven't asked your—your hussy's aid as a matter of course. I know he's on leave. But this is an emergency situation. As a citizen of the Comity, Mrs. Knave, I ask you—"

"Husband," Mirella said. "Hussy is something altogether else, okay? I know, you Earth people don't know a lot about marrying and like that, or anyhow you don't around the Palace. But husband." She took a breath. "An emergency situation. Only Jerry doesn't think so. So I am supposed to think so?"

He did his best with it, and he made it sound as ominous as he could. "Mrs. Knave, Amy-Robsart Berringer has disappeared."

Mirella gave him a small laugh. "You sure?" she said. "How can you tell?"

"Oh, she's a very nice youngster, from all I hear," I said.

"She is nineteen," Mirella said, "she is blonde, she is stacked, and she looks more demure than maybe Snow What. For any male alive, that is guaranteed to be a Very Nice Youngster."

"I tell you," Claude Deke said frantically, "she's gone. Something has to be done."

"And it has to be Jerry to do it, right?" Mirella said. "Because if you let FoFeality at it—that man gives police everywhere a bad name. No, he gives *humans* everywhere a bad name. Anyhow, you let him at it, he will make big-time noise, and he will mess everything up he puts his hands on. So not

FoFeality. So Jerry. Okay, I see it."

"Look, Mirella," I said, "she just didn't show up for the dinner. Or the party. It happens. Claude here—Mirella Knave, Claude Deke—is panicking for no reason."

"Maybe," she said. "And maybe not, too." She looked at me for a second. "Jerry, we have got to stick here a while. Guest of honor, right? So does it hurt, we listen him out? Chances are, you say no and we go away. But, so long as here we are, you got better to listen to?"

TWO

We found a corner nobody was using, and Claude dragged some chairs over. While he was doing that I said: "Mirella, what the Hell do you want to get me involved for?"

She sighed. She has a passionate, fake, operatic sigh. "Because first, no matter what I say, she is not a bad kid. You hear a little, you can tell. And second, maybe one chance in fifty he is right and it is not just ducking a dinner. So if it is that one chance, maybe you can help. Look, if it strings out more than a few days, FoFeality is going to come in, no way to box him off forever. A nice kid, she doesn't deserve that."

Few people, if any, deserve Horace FoFeality. You may not even remember him now—memories are short, just now and then, when the Comity officials want them to be—so let me toss you a fast sketch. Beginning, since you're probably not from Cuchinar (the place is thinly populated, and no wonder), with the damn name.

There's a group on Cuchinar that considers itself an elite. Being one of an elite on Cuchinar is being the ugliest frog I can imagine, in the smallest possible puddle, but there are those, God knows why, who like it. And the Cuchinar elite use Fo—I think it started as From, and shrank from Fro to Fo in positive seconds—the way people, back before the Clean Slate War, used *von* and *de* and all the others. It tells the universe that you have something special and showy in the way of ancestors.

Horace FoFeality was not born on Cuchinar; he was born under Mars Dome, of poor but honest (as they say) parents—at any rate, no prison records have turned up. But as he clambered his unpleasant (but ingratiating) way up the political ladder, he made a few magic passes with this and that Bureau of This and That, and got himself an Ancestry. Plain old Horace Feality became, and has remained, glittering and enviable Horace FoFeality.

It didn't hurt. There are people who don't know much about Cuchinar—most people, in fact, because it's a depressing sort of place to know about—and the odd name gave Horace a little extra interest, and something to be very noisily modest about.

He began his career fixing political machines—vote-counters and displays, automatic yes/no tellers, all that kind of thing. There is always somebody with a brand-new idea about gimmicking such machines, and your average political-machine mechanic gets to be good at brushing them away. Horace, on the other hand, became an expert in the small, shadowy field of Aiding and Abetting.

This led him, because he was a cautious fellow, not to a prison term but to some very fast friendships—stick-tite friendships, in fact—with a few rising local Councillors. And as the Councillors rose, eventually making their way to appointments in the Dichtung, Horace rose, too.

He never stood for an election, naturally. When there were such elections, to make up the short-list from which the Emperor (who does have to stand for elections—and they can be interesting things to stand for, if you've got a lot of patience, and very strong nerves) chooses members of the Dichtung, Horace was bright enough not to be among those present. He was (as I've said) an ingratiating fellow, but he was at his best in small, shadowed corners, inhabited by a maximum of two people.

He became that oddity of government in the Comity, a career Advisor. He Advised a defense minister here, a member for university women there, a group of Councillors hammering out farm policy somewhere else; and if his advice was seldom good, it was always valued, and sometimes, to the dismay of various constituents, actually taken.

Then Roesan Berringer started his second term as Emperor. He'd had a harder time doing that than he'd had getting to his first term; some things had improved over six years, but a fair number had disimproved, and there was a lot of affection building for Willa Smeel, the determined little member for Molar Sciences, NA, who led the Opposition in the Dichtung.

Well, calling it affection may be putting it a little strongly. The general feeling seemed to be: "She might just do better—and, after all, can she do worse?"

Berringer had to call in every favor he had lying around. He called in several from Horace FoFeality, the former expert in gimmicking political machines.

He offered, in return, the post of Governor-General for Cuchinar.

Horace, being familiar enough with Cuchinar—like any

sensible person—at a great distance, suggested Palace Security Chief instead. There is an ancient lyric, long preSpace, that goes:

They wanted *a man who knew the game,*
From serving a lot of time.

Horace had never actually served any time, but he knew the game in the same sort of way; and, to make a long story just a hair shorter, Berringer (on his way to becoming, once more, Roesan I) said to himself: "Why not? What harm can it do?"

He was now—if Claude Deke was right and some trouble had actually erupted—about to find out.

Claude, having returned with the chairs, sketched out, once more, the thin little story he'd told me. Mirella said:

"Jerry is maybe right. It could be she just got bored."

He shook his head. Grimly. "She isn't like that," he said. "She's never missed an occasion like this before. And she wouldn't have missed this one."

"She likes Survivors?"

"She likes Tocks," Deke said. "Knave here has had dealings with them—rather intimate dealings."

Mirella trilled a little laugh. She has a full repertoire of such things, all insanely, and damn charmingly, artificial. "How intimate can you be with a snake?" she said. "But okay, so she likes Tocks, so Jerry knows the King and Queen there. On Haven IV. This is a big thing?"

"For Amy-Robsart," Deke said, "it *is* a big thing. She really wanted to meet Knave. To ask him about the Royal Family—"

"Nassanank and Jessiss," I said. "Nice people. Although not people I understand. Not people any human understands."

"She wouldn't have missed the chance," Deke said. "She—she collects Tock items. Books on them, tapes, artifacts—she owns two *Tock* books, if that's what they are—"

"They look like chandeliers made out of wood," I said. "Or bunches of bananas. You read them by crawling up and down the stalks, from branch one to branch six hundred or so."

"Sounds like fun," Mirella said, and Deke said:

"So you see, Ms.—Mrs. Knave, it isn't just a casual happenstance. If Amy-Robsart Berringer isn't here, it's because something's happened to her."

I sighed. "All right," I said. "Start out. Last seen?"

Mirella reached over and patted my arm. "So you'll do a favor," she said gently. "Probably it will take next to no time, and we'll be out and away someplace more lively."

Mirella is a lovely woman, in her way, and a damn bright one. Every once in a while she is dead wrong. I think I knew, even then, that this was one of those onces.

THREE

Last seen, Claude Deke told us, had been about mid-afternoon, out in the Palace Garden. "She had Security with her, of course."

"Why was she in the garden?" I said.

"No particular reason," he said. "It was quiet there—always is. It's enclosed, natural, no outsiders—she liked it. Likes it, I mean." He gave me a quick grin, and went back to looking worried.

"Doors, walls, fields?"

"The Palace itself encloses it," he said. "There's one stretch—about eight feet long—between buildings, and that's a seven-foot wall. It's not on the official Palace maps—we don't want to spotlight it any. There were plans to build the wall to thirty feet—the buildings on every side are higher—but it's a north wall, and the light's nice."

"Fields?"

"None," he said. "Totally natural environment. Trees, grass, garden paths, flowers—everything does better under natural light and air. Most fields would interfere—with UV radiation, for instance, or rain."

There are some that wouldn't, but they're not common on Earth. No matter, they hadn't been there. "She had Palace Security with her," I said. "Meaning what and who?"

"One agent," he said. "Male. Godney Thrall. Perfectly trustworthy."

I filed the name; I'd file "perfectly trustworthy" when I had some data. "He last saw her in the garden?"

"He was going off shift," Deke said. "Must have been about four o'clock, that's shift change. His relief was late—Martina Greensinger."

Mirella stared. "Hold it," she said. "You are actually telling me—a Security guy, his relief isn't there, and he waltzes out anyhow?"

"It was shift change," Deke said. "They've been used to working that way since—"

"Since FoFeality, don't bother telling me," she said. "The man is a sin and a shame. And six other things I am too damn ladylike to have words for."

"And when this Greensinger got there," I said, "Amy-Robsart was gone."

"She thought the girl had gone to her rooms. Or somewhere around the place. It happens—she didn't think anything of it. Just went back to her duty station and waited for the girl to call her."

"Oh, my God," Mirella said. "This is Security? This is like police work? I would not trust an insect to these people. She doesn't go look, she doesn't call in, she doesn't check back with this Thrall moron?"

"Well," Deke said, uncomfortably, "things *have* been a little lax—"

"Things have been flat, outright horrible," Mirella said. "If it was not serious, it would be a comedy. These Security people could get jobs with the Three Stages. The Mars Brothers."

"Well—"

"She's right," I said. "It's ridiculous. People just sat around staring and whistling. Look: when did anybody actually notice the girl was missing?"

Deke grinned at me again, very briefly. I don't know why; nervousness, maybe. "Her maid—her personal maid—was supposed to meet with her at five-thirty," he said. "To begin preparing her for tonight. When she hadn't appeared in her rooms by six, the maid called Ms. Greensinger. Ms. Greensinger, of course, knew nothing."

"And the maid, being maybe a bright person," Mirella said, "just closed the call off peaceful, and got to you. Or Greensinger would already have got FoFeality mixed in."

"Well," Deke said, "she called Sten Rann. Sten's the Household Subchancellor. He's been with the Palace, on staff, thirty-five years or so—the maid's been here fifteen herself. It was Sten who called me."

"All right," I said, "why you? Why Colonization, for God's sake? Did somebody think the girl had taken off for Kingsley, or Alphacent?"

"Of course not," Deke said. "My God. No. That's not possible." One more fast grin. "But Sten thought—well, you were right here, or you would be tonight. You've handled some odd things, here and there. And you've handled them speedily—and *quietly.* Pupil III, for instance. Even one or two on Earth."

"Not recently," I said, "but it has happened."

Deke smiled again, briefly. "He thought—I might have some influence with you."

"All right," I said. "Fine. You have had some, damn it. I'm going to have to talk to Sten Rann. And Thrall. And this maid—what's her name?"

"Sunny Samuels," he said.

"I'll have to talk to her," I said. "And anybody else who's seen Amy-Robsart today. That's a start, at least." I thought for half a second. "The Emperor," I said. "Does he—"

"He's in Djakarta," Deke said. "The rest of the family—some in Cambridge—did you know there used to be two Cambridges? One in Missichusetts."

"Massatucky," Mirella said. "But that one's gone, the whole state's gone. Any of the family right here in Columbus?"

"No, thank God," Deke said. "They haven't been informed. They'll have to be—but if we can locate Amy-Robsart quickly—"

"Right," I said. "All right, let's start doing that. Without fuss. If I leave now, somebody will wonder why. So Mirella and I will stay right here, and in five seconds—or however short a time you can manage—Sten Rann and Sunny Samuels will wander casually in to do something or other. Plausibly. They'll wander over here, and we'll talk. Thrall's long off duty; he'll wait."

"Thank God, Knave," he said. "You'll find her, won't you?"

"Dead or alive," I said casually, and when I saw his face I wished I hadn't put it that way.

FOUR

Sten Rann came first. By the time he arrived, eight or nine minutes later, Mirella and I were chatting with the Berigot Ambassador, a nice enough Beri named G'dant B'rynter, and a tall, white-haired woman, wearing a great deal of carefully modest and wildly expensive jewelry, who introduced herself as Carola Flake Tomlinson. "You won't have heard of me," she said, in a voice like a bass flute, "but I have certainly heard of you, Mr. Knave. We in the Personal Rights Guild admire your work in the Haven system. Admire it greatly."

It was being a big day for the Tocks of Haven IV. I said something polite, and Mirella said: "You're interested in Tocks?"

"We are interested in upholding the personal rights of all beings," Ms. Tomlinson said, which sounded just a hair too sweeping for me; I am not much, myself, on upholding the personal rights of malignant bacteria, or even a few of the less microscopic life-forms—fire ants, for instance.

"And a good thing, too," Mirella said politely. "Somebody ought to be, I guess. But Tocks look to be doing okay on their own. Help from a Guild, what I hear, they have never needed."

"Ah," Ms. Tomlinson said. "But your—your in-law was a very great help to them, some years ago. He prevented human beings from wiping out the race. The entire indigenous race."

Mirella said: "Husband. In-law is another entire thing," at the same moment I was saying:

"Well, not quite. I prevented human beings from *trying* to exterminate the Tocks." Ms. Tomlinson looked a little baffled by the combination of voices, and G'dant said:

"I had not heard of your association with the Tocks, Knave. You make a fascinating distinction."

By then the woman had got things sorted out. To Mirella she said: "But it *is* a legal relationship, isn't it? Surely in-law—" She made a sketchy sort of gesture, and she turned to me without waiting for a reply. "Well," she said, "had they been allowed to try, the Tocks would have been wiped out, of course. It comes to the same thing."

I let Mirella have first crack. "It's legal," she said. "Husband and wife is legal. Emperor and Councillor is also legal. But in-laws they are not, except maybe very special circumstances."

"Quite so," G'dant said. Then, to Ms. Tomlinson: "What Knave appears to be saying, Madam, is that humans might not, in fact, have succeeded in their aim. Tock resistance might have been—overwhelming."

That idea, clearly, had never occurred to her before. She was still considering it (or considering the idea of Tocks having in-laws; who can tell?) when I noticed a square-jawed fellow with short grey hair looking uncomfortable just behind her. Not very uncomfortable—he was doing his best to seem plausibly natural—but I gave him a smile, and said: "Oh, Mr. Rann. There's something I've been meaning to ask you."

The Tomlinson woman turned around, saw a Palace servitor, and turned right back. "The Tocks, surely—" she began.

"Sorry," I said. "Let's meet later, shall we? You can tell me all about the Tocks. But I can't expect to find Mr. Rann unoccupied for long, and I've got to take advantage. You'll understand."

G'dant said: "B'russ'r sends his regards and his good wishes for you, and for your mate and partner. Odd and lonely to own only two sexes, but humans seem to have adjusted to the scarcity."

Berigot have four—two He and two She. I thanked him, and by extension B'russ'r B'dige, whom I'd met a couple of years before on Ravenal. "I really do have to talk to Mr. Rann," I said. "I'm sorry—maybe we'll get another chance later on."

"I should be delighted," he said, and we hissed politely at each other and tilted heads—he left, I right. When he started to wander off, Ms. Tomlinson followed him, a little vague in her motions. Too much champagne, too many jewels, or too much Guild, I couldn't be sure which.

Mirella turned her head. "You're Sten Rann?" she said. "Nice to meet you. Come on, we'll find chairs."

We'd moved a little away from our corner, but when we got back the chairs were still there and still empty; it wasn't really a sit-down sort of crowd. More a milling-and-murmuring bunch.

We got Sten Rann seated—he sat a little stiffly, here at a

party full of glittering people, or whatever the Hell they were—in the middle, Mirella on his left. I said: "You do know what this is about?"

"Amy-Robsart," he said. "I mean—Ms. Berringer."

"Where do you think she might be?" I said, keeping it fairly casual, and hoping he'd come up with some plausible spot.

"Anywhere," he said. "She doesn't just go off like this. It's disturbing. Nobody notified me till—my God, till about six-fifteen. By then a couple of hours had gone by."

"You don't keep tabs on her yourself," I said.

"Not my job, and no need," he said. "I tend to leave it to Security—and I should damn well have known better. These last few years—well, Palace Security's not what it was."

"We know," Mirella said. "The idiot in charge, right?"

"Well," Sten Rann said mildly, "I wouldn't really call him an idiot, Mrs. Knave. He's really quite clever, on his own ground. But Palace Security isn't his ground, is what it is."

"So he should be at least bright enough to know that," Mirella said. "Somebody gave me a job leading an orchestra, I would at least know it was not my job."

He shrugged. "In any case," he said, "I don't have much to contribute. Not yet. I will have—whatever happened left traces. Traces can be found."

"Right," Mirella said, and I said:

"Were there any indications—small ones, things you might not have noticed much at the time—of any trouble, or any cause for trouble? She's nineteen—a romance? An impatience with Imperial life?"

"Look," he said. "This is private, isn't it? It had better be. There is a romance. But there's no trouble about it. It's just that people don't know yet. Nobody knows—oh, I do. Sunny does. If the Security people were on their toes, they'd know too, probably. But I doubt it like Hell—and nobody else knows."

"Except, possibly, the other party," I said. "Who?"

He shrugged. "Got to tell you. It'll come to nothing, but I've got to open up everything. No other way you can work. He's a young kid who hangs around the place. Guy Finch."

Mirella said: "You know, Sten, I like you. You think clear. And right." And I said:

"Finch? Any relation to an Astarte Finch?"

"Don't judge the kid by his mother," Sten said. "Not this time. She's—well, if you're building idiots, you can use her for your prototype."

She'd seemed all of that when I'd talked to her, just before Claude Deke had come along. But then, I'd seen her, probably, not at her best.

"But her son—Guy—is different?" I said.

Sten shut his eyes for a second. When he opened them he said: "I know what you want, and here it is, very quick. Guy Finch, 22, hair very blond, eyes dark yellow. Like a cat's eyes. Maybe six-two, six-three, real thin, walks in a slouch. Wears glasses for reading, horn-rimmed, and he's always reading. Or carrying something—book, news sheets, magazine. Graduated from a good Scholarte—Yarvard. Their history goes back before the Clean Slate War, when it used to be two schools, but of course it had to move; one of the old schools was totally destroyed, and the other wasn't in much better shape. They're in New Mexico now, but still full of tradition. Why am I talking about a Scholarte?"

"Because you don't know what else to say," I told him. "You're filling in any facts you can grab while you hunt for the right ones."

"I suppose," he said. "He's a good kid, you know? He wouldn't—whatever it is happened, it's not him."

I nodded. "What did he study at Yarvard?"

"Some kind of biophysics," he said. "Virtual echo structures, something like that. Clone states."

Which meant very little to me just then. I was just collecting facts; you never know which ones are going to be valuable, so you get all you can, and sort things out later. Mirella said:

"The family—they didn't know about this Guy? You know, her maid knows, but not the family?"

"It can work that way," he said. "Hard to keep anything hidden from the people who work close around you, right? But the family—this is a nineteen-year-old girl, they know what she wants them to know."

She nodded. "So if they did know," she said, "would they make a fuss? I mean, he is just this Finch's kid, not like he is something special."

"Well," Sten Rann said, "Finch's kid *is* something special. I mean, Astarte Finch is a big name around here."

"We're strangers," I said. "I know more about the setup on Ravenal, or Kingsley, than I do about the one on Earth."

"Right," Mirella said. "Look, Sten: what is it makes her name so big? A husband—well, a companion, whatever it is here—with influence? With money, maybe?"

"He died maybe eighteen years ago," he said. "Maybe twenty. When Guy was real little. He had cash, sure—family goes way back around Columbus, over a hundred years—and she inherited. What she did with the cash was, she made a spot for herself around politics."

"She's a Councillor?" I said.

"Not hardly," he said. "But she knows Councillors. She throws parties. For some people it's a life's work, throwing parties. You set up the right kind, you invite the right people, you get influence. People talk to you, people listen to you."

"Hostessing," Mirella said. "Even on Ravenal we got some of it, not a lot. A famous hostess, she is like the power behind things. You handle it right, you can do a lot with some champagne and some fancy crackers."

"Political hostess," I said. "All right: does she specialize?"

"Specialize how?"

"One party in the Dichtung? One kind of political cause? Law people, or advisors, or influence-peddlers?"

"Or," Mirella said, "Security types? FoFeality, maybe?"

He shrugged. "The whole barrel," he said. "Take your pick. She's not much on causes—whatever's fashionable, nothing pushed for too long, nothing she wants to lean on. She goes for the influential people—Councillors, Judges, the Imperial family and household, the opinion people. FoFeality, sure—he's tied in sixty ways to six hundred people. Or—say somebody comes up with a discovery in molar physics, or a big new book of poetry, or an art show someplace expensive—she'll throw a party for that, too. Some of them are impressed with being guests of honor. Some know better—nothing personal, Knave."

"Nothing personal," I agreed. "I do know better—but you don't refuse an Imperial invitation. Not at all polite."

"Sure," he said. "You've been places. All kinds of places. It's a chance we don't get, around here."

FIVE

The rule goes back to Walther IV, who is generally tagged as the first real Emperor of the Comity, quite a ways back. There have been exceptions, but it takes a screaming Comity-wide emergency to create one.

The Emperor stays on Earth. All the time. He may—if nothing's happening, if everybody agrees, if there's no tiny objection anywhere—spend a day or so on the Moon. Once or twice.

It's the price he pays for being Emperor, I suppose. He travels all over the planet, visiting everything from the ruins of Seattle to the interesting (they tell me) bustle of Sydney—and though he has a home base in the Imperial Palace, in Columbus, Ohio, NA, he isn't tied down that tightly.

But he doesn't leave the planet. It sounds as limiting as Hell, until you remind yourself that, for most of human history, nobody did. They managed to get along all right, and they don't seem to have felt much more bored or confined than people seem to feel now.

I gave him a grin. "The household follows the rule?"

"We go where the family goes," he said. "Where they don't—we don't. It's all right. It's a life."

"Wait a minute," Mirella said. "So this Finch is a somebody. Okay. So still there could be objections. There is all kinds somebodies, and one somebody could hate some other somebody. It happens."

He shook his head. "No objections," he said. "There are people—the Darren crowd, maybe—who think of Astarte Finch as a lightweight—more cash than brains. There are jokes. But that's just one crowd, really—well, mostly—and for the family—well, the kind of brains Bob Darren and those people have, you don't look for it in an Emperor."

"So for the family, this Guy kid would be okay?" she said.

"As far as I can see, sure," he said. "And it might just peter out, after all. Though I don't think so—these quiet ones, they find somebody, they tend to stick. And Guy Finch is a quiet kind of kid himself. Naturally enough, I suppose."

"Okay," I said. "Let's look somewhere else. Friends. Interests."

He grinned at me. "You're scouting for trouble," he said, "and there isn't any. She was tight with her father. She could get to him any time, and she'd tell him things. How so-and-so was really a good guy, how something-or-other was really a bad idea. Youngest kid, you know how it can be; Roesan would always make time for her. Listen to her. Once in a while, maybe, take the advice."

"Trouble there could still be," Mirella said.

"I guess," he said, "but there isn't. If you looked around here for the last person to be in any kind of mess about any kind of thing, Amy-Robsart would be it, no contest."

"So," I said, "the likeliest thing is that nothing's happened."

"No," he said. "The likeliest thing is, somebody put the snatch on her. You don't have to make trouble to get kidnapped—all you have to do is be is the wrong person in the wrong spot. An Imperial kid—somebody might be thinking ransom. Or pressure, maybe."

"A dangerous way to think," I said. "Police everywhere would start looking—and some Earth police might be pretty good. FoFeality can't be a fair sample."

"Some people," he said, "*do* dangerous kinds of things. Once in a long while, some of them get away with it, too."

It was the next afternoon before Amy-Robsart Berringer came back. She was unharmed, she was apologetic about a sudden call to go sailing with some distant friends off what remains of the Florida Keys, and it was perfectly clear to everybody that she hadn't been kidnapped, or hit over the head, or anything else.

That was when the trouble *really* started.

SIX

"The fact is," I told Mirella, two nights later—we were undressing, back in my Columbus digs, after (for a change) a quiet night with actual friends—"something happened. Something distinctly unpleasant."

"Something," she said, and worked her way out of a dark-green dress that looked good on her, though not as good as Mirella looked without it. "That far I will go. But why unpleasant? The kid does not look scared, she does not look like shock, she does not jump when something goes bang. Everybody says she was a quiet kid, and she is a quiet kid."

"But not the same quiet kid," I said, and hung up my shirt. The dress code around Columbus is, as you'd expect, both rigid and old-fashioned.

"Okay," she said. "Still with you that far. Everybody says— she is like changed. A lot changed."

"But it's how she's changed that points at the unpleasantness," I said. "Memory lapses. Slow responses—hesitations, anyhow. It's not shock—all right—but what causes things like that except some kind of massive hit?"

"Trauma effect, right," she said. She sat down in an overstuffed dark-brown chair, and I went to the big leather one I usually sat in when actually at home. "That's how we learned it, police school. Something bad happens to you, you are going anyhow to show traces. Some people cry, some people get mad."

"And some act just like Amy-Robsart," I said. She nodded.

"So okay," she said. "Unpleasant. I wonder where she was."

"Out sailing," I said. "Florida Keys." Mirella gave me a scornful laugh, one of her better numbers.

"I would sooner believe out sailing in the Sahara," she said. "The big question is, how can we find out?"

"I've got a better one," I said. "Why should we? Nobody's asking us, not now. She's back—and people are a little worried about her, but give it three weeks and nobody will remember what the worry was about. Sten Rann will relax, Claude Deke's *already* relaxed—why should we bother?"

"You're kidding, right?" she said.

I sighed. "Damn it, I guess I am," I said. "If something did happen—maybe it's not through happening. Whatever it was, maybe there's more to it. And if that's true—"

"Then the guy on the spot, the guy who'll handle, will be Horace FoFeality," Mirella said. "Who nobody deserves: believe it." She shook her head. "This is a good kid," she went on. "When we met her a couple of days after the dinner, she listened to you tell her a couple of Tock stories, and she listened good for all five minutes, and she's interested. Maybe not as much as people said, but interested. In something besides herself and the Palace. I get the feeling this is not such a common thing to be, you're part of the Imperial family."

"She is a good kid," I said. "But—all right, we want to help. How do we find a way in?"

Mirella never hesitated. "Only one good way in," she said. "The family—no. Why start things off by worrying them? People panic, maybe even Imperial people panic. Who needs it? Sten Rann, anybody in the household, same story; by them, it's all smooth now. So let it stay smooth."

I looked at her. "That doesn't leave much," I said.

"It leaves anyhow two people," she said, "and we can work them together." I took a second with it, and then grinned at her.

"Hell of a couple they'd make," I said.

"You never know," she said. "Look at us. Big and small, thin and round. But we'll make it okay."

"We will at that," I said. "But—Claude Deke and Astarte Finch."

She saw the grin leave my face. "I know," she said. "It is work, and it is going to be hard work and careful work. And you figured you were through with everything for a while."

"Well," I said, "we're celebrating. First of all, I promised you a celebration back on Ravenal—"

"That was a year ago," she said. "That one, we had."

"Second, we've been married—what? Five weeks. Five small weeks."

"Five weeks two days," she said. "So it's time, maybe, to get moving again." She held out her arms. "Come over here, Jerry," she said. "So I'll hold you a little, and it'll be okay."

And the fact is, it was okay.

It's a gift, and for me Mirella has it. She will never make

heads turn when we walk into somewhere or other—and I have made a small, pleasant career out of escorting rosebuds who make heads not only turn but positively spin like tops. She is a small round woman with a mop of tightly curled black hair on top of her head, and she manages somehow to be both kind and realistic, always, which is a trick I have never seen pulled off before. We met while I was digging into some oddities on Ravenal and she was a police Lance-Corporal there—I've put most of that into a report somewhere or other—and a month or less after we'd met we went off in my ship for Earth and celebration, and a while after what some preSpace poet calls, for some damn reason, "that first, fine, careless rupture", she was somebody I would have bet large money would never exist: Mrs. Mirella Knave.

That is, if I could have found anybody who'd have taken what turned out to be the winning side of that particular bet. Those who know me, more or less, were pretty well universally sure that, while I might end up dead, or mad, or broke, or (on the other hand) offensively rich and happy, I was not going to end up married.

But I have, and Mirella is the reason for it, because after I had been around her for a small while nothing else made any sense at all.

And when I am around her now, things do make sense. Even things like Claude Deke, Astarte Finch and the Mystery of the Slightly Missing Princess.

It's a gift.

SEVEN

Claude Deke was going to be a small problem, but Astarte Finch was no problem at all. Mirella suggested an addition I wasn't sure would work, but she was confident.

"You invite her here, she is going to come," she said. "No way not. For eight minutes you are a somebody, and for a hostess-type no way even to duck. You invite her to bring her little boy, she is going to put him in a cage and get him dragged here if she has to."

"I like it," I said, "and I'm going to have to meet Guy. But—say she wants to trap me into a party or an appearance or something. Why would she want her son along? And he's not a little boy, he's taller than I am."

"By Astarte Finch, he'll be a little boy when he is ninety-three," she said, "and maybe eight feet tall. I know the type: believe it. People talk; I listen."

"Okay," I said. "So you do."

"And not only a little boy," Mirella said. "*Her* little boy. She will come up here, she will wear every jewel she can locate around her place, and she will wear her little boy, because he is one more jewel. Wait and see."

"Mother love," I said.

"Nothing like," she said. "Love of being a mother—maybe. And even that, just maybe. But there are people—they own something, it does not even have to be special. It is special because *they own it*. And first on the list of stuff they own is other people: kids and—what is it here?—companions especially."

We set it up the next day, for two days ahead—it isn't a good idea to rush a hostess, it makes her nervous and suspicious. Meanwhile, Mirella said she'd poke around the Imperial household staff a little—just being a curious, slightly privileged, tourist. She's good at that; she looks interested, and people tell her things. She said it: people talk, and she listens. It works.

And I set out after Claude Deke.

He was, as I've said, a small problem.

I'd told him, after all, and with certainty, that I wasn't working for Colonization. While he'd thought he needed me, that hadn't mattered, but it was going to matter now: he had no special need to come and see me, and, as far as I could see, no special desire either.

But if I told him I'd sign on again for active duty, there I'd be—long after whatever was going to happen to Amy-Robsart Berringer had happened—stuck with a paying job. Not at all what I wanted.

Well, I realized, there is No, and there is Yes, and there is also flirtation. So, after I'd been as charming as was even slightly reasonable to Astarte Finch, I punched up the local Colonization offices—the main business quarters are in Grand Forks, Idaho, where almost everything except the Palace is, but of course there's a Columbus suite—and carefully didn't ask for Claude Deke.

I went from the mech secretarials to a cheery young woman named Freilah Schussmann, who was calmly willing to chat with me about new developments, drone-ship reports, assignments open, and so on, once she was sure I was me. I listened to four or five minutes of that, a little of it about the successes of other Survivors, and a lot of it about three planets the drones had reported on, all of them up for assignment.

"One of them looks *very* interesting," she said. "It's a G6 star, which makes it just a bit odd—but there's something else that really makes it unusual."

"Tell me about it," I said. Truth to tell, I was interested— not interested enough to sign on for the job, God knows—I'd spent enough days, a Standard year at a time, living alone on new planets, either in order to prove that human beings could survive on them, or establish that they damn well couldn't— but interested. Slightly. As a spectator.

"Well," she said, "I don't know all that much about it, myself. Let me connect you with the person who's got the data."

Jackpot, I thought, but what I said was: "Isn't it all on computer?"

"Naturally," she said. "But it's simpler if you know just what to access for all the different angles, isn't it?"

"I suppose it is," I said, having, I thought, sounded reluctant enough to be persuasive. She told me to hold on, and clicked off. After fifteen seconds a mech told me, as they do: "You have not been disconnected." After thirty seconds it told me again.

Thirty-eight seconds of waiting. Well, two could flirt as well as one. Then there was a small click and Claude Deke said:

"Knave? Is that you?"

"It is," I said. "Claude Deke?"

"At your service," he lied. "You've been asking about Holly?"

"Holly," I said. "That's the odd planet off a G6?"

"Odd enough," he said. "I'm understating it when I say we've never run into one like this before."

"All right," I said, "tell me about it."

He chuckled. He had a very bad false chuckle. "Knave," he said, "why would you be interested? The job will go to some active Survivor—Bruno Carr, like as not."

Carr is a barely-competent Survivor—below barely-competent there are no Survivors, not among the living—with bad manners, no taste and reflexes just fast enough to get him out of the trouble he keeps making for himself. "Well, let's say I'm curious," I said. "It's something to think about, while I'm on leave."

"It won't wait long," he said. "They never do, you know that."

"Even so—" I said, and he bit.

"Why don't I stop by and fill you in?" he said. "I could bring charts and printout—you'll really want the details on this one."

"Well," I said, "I've got things to do, the next day or so." And we set a time—an hour after the expected arrival of Astarte Finch and Son.

Bruno Carr?

Well, if the man's long run of luck was finally going to run out on Holly, whatever the Hell it was, why should I care?

The Hell with him.

EIGHT

Two days with nothing to do—except hunt and fish, so to speak. Mirella was doing a lot of background, chatting with Palace people and the like, and I'd be getting her reports, which are good, but there was another angle. Or rather two angles. The Palace Garden was one; maybe Amy-Robsart had just wandered away and been lured off, and maybe she'd been grabbed right from the Garden—in which case, as Mirella and Sten Rann had agreed, there'd be traces. After all this damn time. Maybe.

And then there was the other angle. Maybe he knew nothing at all—and I certainly hoped so—but I had the time, and you never do know. It was very late afternoon when I found him, where I'd expected to find him—not in his offices, not hard at work, but playing semicomputer billiards at one of his clubs. I don't know how many clubs Horace FoFeality belonged to— my guess would be fifty-three, all of them gamely putting up with the ingratiating little weasel—but he was said to favor I. D. K., a very exclusive place whose initials were supposed to stand for something very secret. When a member was asked what the initials meant, he (or she, or whatever term applies; the membership includes a few Berigot and one Kelan) invariably said: "I don't know." It's surprising, in a way, how many people didn't get it.

It's a nice place—an old-fashioned, dark-wood set of rooms. I'm not a member—I'm not much for club life, because you seldom meet anybody in a club you didn't expect to meet—but G'dant B'rynter was, and he was nice enough to get me in as a guest. We had half an hour of chat about mutual friends, and then I spotted FoFeality and told G'dant my job had begun.

"Job?" he said. "I knew that you had a purpose in asking me to invite you, Knave, but—"

"Well, maybe it's a job," I said. "Non-paying, but I'm on leave anyhow. I'll fill you in when I can." And I was off to kibitz on the semic. billiards game.

It's a fascinating game, if you like unexpected frustration. Fifteen balls, a table, six pockets—just like preSpace billiards, except that the balls, when hit, go as expected only some of the time. The table is crisscrossed with small fields, which change with every third shot, and change unpredictably. The fields are invisible, of course; you find out one's there when your ball (or a ball yours has hit) smacks into it and either rebounds or slides along it at a new and surprising angle.

The field locations and types are not supposed to be predictable, though every player has his own set of ideas about periodicity and pattern. I did have a feeling that FoFeality, an expert in other sorts of machinery, had a private way to gimmick the computers that created and blanked the fields—but it was only a feeling, and based on nothing more than his dingy little reputation. I stood by and watched him take a shot, watched his opponent—a hulking fellow with a great deal of white hair, and a blank, though slightly grim, expression—take a shot, and watched Horace take another.

He's a tiny man shaped like a miniature barrel, with small hands and feet and a large, ball-shaped nose on a dark, sweaty face. His mouth is a small, straight line, his black, severe eyebrows move up and down quite a lot, and his greying hair shoots up here and there in tufts and small clumps. The second shot I saw him take hit a field, slid along it, kissed the nine ball and rolled it into an end pocket.

"Very nice," I said, as the table lit up for half a second—field change.

"I saw the ghost of it on Hammermill's shot," he said, staring at the table. His voice is a slightly hoarse little mumble. "If it hadn't been there, I'd have scratched."

Hammermill frowned down at the table. He bent, thought for a second, and took his shot. The ball smacked into the three, rebounded, hit a field and smacked the three again, very quickly, going away. Hammermill's ball caromed off toward the ten, sitting on the rail, and the three slid toward a side pocket, hit another field and bounced off, stopping about a foot from where it had started.

"Bad luck," I said. Hammermill grunted. FoFeality said:

"There's always a field around the left side pocket after the fourth angle field. Or the third. Depends, depends, but you have to allow for it."

He took his own shot, and sank the ten.

I made a few more casual comments, and the game slowly

wound to a finish. Hammermill said: "You're awfully good at this," when he'd lost, and FoFeality said:

"Memory and wrist, that's the whole game. All of it: memory and wrist. That's it." He looked up at me. "Like to try your hand?" he said.

Hammermill was putting his cue away. I said: "I don't play often—don't get the chance."

Horace grinned at me. "Have to make time," he said. "Have to, don't you know? Relaxation's important—can't allow yourself to wither down to a dry stick, something like that. A dry stick. No. When you're between jobs, you should make time. All work and no play, after all. All work. Not the best thing, now, is it?"

"Well, I'm not on Earth all that often," I said. "And the game's not really established on many other worlds."

"A shame," he said. "Shame. It ought to be." He racked the balls, and I got a cue. We exchanged names, and I said:

"FoFeality? You're from Cuchinar?"

"My ancestors," he said vaguely. The preen was just visible. "I've made a small spot for myself here—with the Palace, you know. Palace work, it's where I've found a niche. Satisfying, in its way." Another small preen; it was mostly in the eyebrows, and the shoulders. "I think I've heard *your* name."

I nodded. I took the first shot, and sank nothing. "I was up at the Palace the other night," I said. "A small dinner, nothing showy."

"Ah, yes," he said. "The Survivor. Indeed. Gerald Knave. I have heard the name, then, indeed I have. An exciting sort of life. It would be that, I suppose?"

"It has its moments," I said, and watched him sink the twelve, skidding it off a small field to drop into a side pocket.

Well, there's no use detailing the game; I sat back and let Horace win it handily. There's a little more to it than memory and wrist, of course—the technique is to take your shots so that, if no field interferes, you're good one way, and if one does you have a fair chance at being good another way—but I played the kind of blunt, straight-ahead game Hammermill had played, making Horace feel as comfortable as I could.

When we'd finished, he said: "For a novice, you're not at all bad. A novice, you know, but promising. Distinctly promising.

You should try to make time—try to practice more, you know."

"I might be able to, now," I said. "I've gone on a long leave—and about time, too. I'd like to stay around Columbus a while—see the sights, that kind of thing."

"Not much adventure in that, now, for a Survivor," he said. "Can't be."

"Oh, there's always something," I said, just as casually. "The night of that little dinner, there *was* some excitement."

"Sorry to have missed it," he said. "Very sorry. An exciting dinner—distinctly an odd moment, wouldn't you say?"

"I understand there was some worry over Amy-Robsart," I said.

He nodded. "Came to nothing, didn't it?" he said. "She never did turn up just then—well, Imperial affairs can be pretty wearing, you know. Pretty wearing." Another tiny preen. "But she'd just gone off sailing—something like that, sailing away. Found a friend or two, and went off into the blue, you know. Came back perfectly fine, perfectly fine. She'll be more careful now. Count on it." He gave me a little smile. It tried to be a pleasant one, but not nearly hard enough.

"I suppose she might at that," I said.

"I'm sure of it," he said. "Sure. She'll be careful. And it'll be good for everyone that way. Much better, in fact—much better in all sorts of ways." He gave me another quick, unpleasant smile. "She'll be just fine," he said. "You can count on it. Just fine."

"Well," I agreed, "it *was* only one more dinner, for the Emperor's daughter. And she did turn up the next day."

He chuckled. He had a low, grating chuckle. "Tell the truth of it," he said, "I was just a bit surprised to be told she'd gone sailing. It did surprise me, you know. I rather expected she'd gone off—well, gone off with young Finch somewhere."

I looked puzzled. Faintly. "Young Finch?"

"Well, no one's supposed to know about this, you know," he said. "But there's something there Something between the youngsters. In my job, you get to know all the little details about people. *All* the details; and very handy it is, too." His little eyes glittered when he grinned. "Very handy indeed," he said.

"Your job?" I said, and let him tell me. I nodded and looked as impressed as I thought plausible.

"It's a terrible responsibility, simply terrible," he finished, and I said:

"Sounds as if it would be. You've got to keep very close tabs on everything."

He gave me another unpleasant little grin. "There's not much escapes me, Mr. Knave," he said. "Not much at all. At least, not much having to do with the Palace. Oh, it's dull work compared with yours, I'm sure, very dull—but the Emperor appreciates its importance. Indeed he does."

"I appreciate it myself," I said. "I mean, suppose something *had* happened to Amy-Robsart."

"I'd have been right on it," he said, and gave me one more bright unpleasant grin. "Right *on* it. You can count on that, Mr. Knave. I don't let grass grow under my feet, you know."

If it wanted to, I am damned if I know how anybody would stop it. But I nodded and said something vague and polite, and I went away.

I had some news now, and maybe Mirella would have some, too.

NINE

Mirella had large baskets full of news, none of it immediately worth much—though there were possibilities. She'd talked to Sten Rann again, just casually renewing an acquaintance, gossiping about the Palace in a mild way—and getting, she told me, "the very good idea that something has happened. Not that he's worried—Rann, I mean."

"Something has happened, he knows it's happened, and he's not worried?" I said.

"Amy-Robsart," she said, "is being very Responsible. Keeping him informed. Keeping everybody informed. She does not so much as burp, she tells somebody about it. I think it's got him puzzled, but not worried. Responsible is good, and good is all he wants to know."

I nodded. "Well," I said, "she threw a scare into people when she—whatever she did. Went off somewhere. Now she's being careful not to do that again."

"Could be," Mirella said, "if she went off on her own and came back on her own—which is not likely. If something pushed her, which is more likely by maybe fifty thousand times—so why be just careful and responsible? Why not first tell somebody at least a name, for instance who pushed you?"

"True," I said. "But—"

"There's more," she said. "There's Guy Finch. All of a sudden, she is not seeing Guy Finch."

"All of a sudden," I said, and thought about it. "They've broken up?"

"Not a break," she said. "More a fade. Like they say hello, they are not mad at each other, but they are not much of anything else, either."

"This is the way Sten Rann sees it?"

Mirella nodded. "What Guy Finch thinks, he has no idea, and why should he care? But from what he sees, Amy-Robsart has cooled off. A lot, and sudden."

So far, we were looking at confirming data: interesting, but not very. But Mirella had talked to Sunny Samuels, too, Amy-Robsart's personal maid.

"And this Sunny," she said, "I want you to see. There is

something there, and something weird. What she thinks, or what she's afraid about, or what she knows, I have not got one single idea."

"But?" I said.

"But there is something," she said. "And you'll do better with her than I am ever going to do. I am not a hero Survivor, I am not a five-minute celebrity—and I am not male."

I nodded again. "So we'll set up something," I said. "We'll talk."

Mirella grinned at me. "I got it set up," she said.

She had, too. Amy-Robsart was interested in Tocks; I'd had some dealings with Tocks, and had even told her a few fast stories about that; I could find a nice surprise for the girl. "You got *something*, right?" Mirella said. "I mean, a Tock book, a picture maybe, an autograph? Something you could hand off to Amy-Robsart, make a good gift for an Emperor's daughter?"

There had to be something, and there was: in my ship, in stasis, there were still a few pounds of coffee, a gift from Nassanank and Jessiss. The Tocks—some of them—like coffee, and are fairly good with it, and their Palace (which is in a city called London, on Haven IV—well, a Tock city, not much like Earth's London, or for that matter much like Columbus, Ohio) stocks a blend I'd grown fond of over a few visits.

I'd cheerfully sacrifice a pound in a good cause, and this did seem like a good cause. "I'll have to go and get the stuff," I said.

"That," Mirella said, "you can do later. I know you and ships—no good sending a messenger to get the coffee, you have to go there in person."

"If anybody else tries to get in," I said, "he'll blow himself up. If he gives it a real, hard try, he'll blow part of the ship up too. Simpler to run my own errands, and keep the ship secure."

"Well, later will do," Mirella said. "Sunny will come by, you'll arrange delivery, how and when, so then you'll have a chance to talk."

"When's she due?" I said, and Mirella checked her watch.

"Twelve minutes, if she's on time," she said. "A personal maid to the daughter of an Emperor, so I will bet an on-time type."

She was ninety seconds early. And I agreed with Mirella at

once: there was definitely something there, behind the face.

Sunny Samuels was a reasonably large woman in her early fifties, with a very calm face and a slightly nervous manner. That was a fair opening tipoff. True, there are lots of people whose faces look calm, and who seethe inwardly, and show it only a little.

But they usually show it not just in manner but in topography: their faces are full of little lines, the corners of their eyes have radiating small furrows attached, the twin creases that can either be smile or frown lines, depending, are very marked.

Sunny Samuels had a face as unlined as a baby's. Her skin was smooth, pale, slightly damp porcelain, her hands just as pale and almost as unlined. She didn't look like a Palace personal maid, she looked like a fairly good domestic cook. Her hair was a little thin, a very light brown, and just curly enough to be a bother instead of an attraction. Her eyes were a washed-out blue.

She wore a ring I recognized as a Security seal, which made me wonder just a little; Horace FoFeality—among his other bejewelments—had been wearing one, too. Her only other adornment was a limp-looking thin chain around her neck, probably gold.

And she was nervous not by temperament—no topography for it—but (obviously) because she was talking to me.

"Mr. Knave," she said, in a voice two inches from whine, and an inch and a half from soprano. "It's a pleasure to meet you. Your whiff has been telling me so much about you. You've had such an *exciting* career."

"Wife," Mirella said. With an edge. We were all sitting down in the living room of my place, Mirella in the overstuffed chair she seems to have adopted, me in my own chair and Sunny Samuels, by invitation, on a small pale-brown sofa, two shades darker than her hair. Her hands fiddled with each other in her lap. Not much.

"Yes," she said, and turned back to me as if I'd been the North Magnetic Pole. "I understand you have something you want to present to Ms. Berringer." She batted her eyes at me. I was male.

"Well," I said, "I know she's interested in Tocks. We had

quite a chat about them, after she got back."

She gave me a smile. A female smile. It was a fair attempt. "Oh," she said. "From sailing. Yes, she does like to sail."

"So I understand," I said. "I'm sorry to have missed her at the dinner the other night, but I do understand—the attraction of a catamaran can be overpowering."

"Catamaran," she said. "Yes. You mean the boat."

"I suppose you've gone sailing with her quite a lot," I said. "It must be a fascinating hobby."

"She's quite good," she said. Mirella was doing one of the things she does best—quietly, unobtrusively watching for details. I do it myself—in a way it's my life's work—but it's nice to have a check on your eye. And any woman will see things about another woman (and sometimes about a man) that any man is going to miss. "Do you know much about sailing, Mr. Knave?"

"Knave," I said, and she nodded.

"Of course. Knave." The eyes again.

"Not a thing," I lied. "I get seasick, I'm afraid."

"Oh," she said. The relaxation was just perceptible. "It's really a lot of fun," she said. "Running before the wind, putting the sails up and taking them down—it's wonderful exercise. I go out with her a lot, of course."

"She's been doing it for years, I suppose," I said, knowing the answer.

"She's just taken it up," Sunny said. "But she's a very quick learner—and of course I've had to learn a lot, too, I'm with her so much. She's a fine sailor, and she does love it so. Though I understand she's—gone just a little off it, since her return." The smile again. We were old, old friends. If possible something more. "Well," she said, "young people and their fads. Easy come and easy go."

"Were you with her this trip?" I said.

The smile looked a little calmer this time. "Oh, no," she said. "She just went off on her own. She's not supposed to—but young folk will cut up, you know." She gave me an understanding look, female to male.

"Just decided to head for her boat," I said.

"The catamaran," she said. "Yes."

"They must be hard to handle," I said. "Just a tiny single-hulled ship, in a rough sea—" I shrugged.

"Oh, yes, they are tiny, and the hull," she said. "She's assured me about the hull, you know, we've gone over it in detail. But she's very good, she truly is. I don't have to do too much, when we go sailing together, not really. Though of course I'm always ready. And there wasn't a storm or anything this time, was there?"

"I understand she's promised to behave, from now on," I said.

She looked at me with a little, maternal smile. She really wasn't bad. "Oh, she'll behave," she said. "She does understand that she worried people. She's quite good about things like that, once she does realize. And—in point of fact—I think she's—gone off sailing now."

I nodded. "Well," I said, "I've got something the Tocks gave me—a special coffee blend used in their Palace. I could arrange to present her with a pound of it."

One more smile. "Oh, she'd love that, I'm sure," she said. "If you'd like to present it in person, that might be arrangeable—but there would be some delay, I'm afraid. Her schedule's very full."

I returned the smile. "I'm in no hurry," I said. "And she might like to have it direct from me—the only person besides the Tocks who's touched it."

"Well, it might really be some time—"

"I understand," I said, and she gave it up.

"I'm sure," she said. "Is it here? In your home, I mean?"

"On my ship," I said. "But I can arrange to get it and deliver it, if we can fix a time."

So we fixed one. And after she'd gone, Mirella said: "Wow."

"Wow indeed," I said. "She's not bad—she got 'catamaran' and filed it right. But she relaxed too fast. And she was a little too fancy about the hull."

"What was that?" she said. "I missed it."

"Amy-Robsart told her about the hull," I said. "In detail. And it's not a single hull, not on a catamaran. It's a double hull. Much safer, much larger, and much more seaworthy."

Mirella nodded. "So aha," she said. "So also, some day you will have to take me on a sail. That I have never done, and who knows? It could be fun, if you don't drown."

"Some day," I said. "And then there was the Security ring."

"Security," Mirella said with scorn. "Nervous, shaky, and she gives away too much. This FoFeality is ruining a good operation—or I hope he is. I hope Security was better before he took over."

I nodded. "It must have been," I said. "The Palace hasn't burned down yet." I took a deep breath. "All right," I said. "What do we know?"

TEN

"We know she's lying about the sailing trip," Mirella said. "But that, we knew beforehand."

"The catamaran, right," I said. "Sunny may have gone sailing once or twice with Amy-Robsart. Running before the wind—she's read a book about it, anyhow."

"And the nerves," Mirella said. "She makes her play for you—okay, she figures to do that, and she has to know people figure her that way, so she makes it. But a fake play, she's pressing too hard with me right here in the room. Right?"

"Right," I said, considering it. "And Amy-Robsart's not sailing any more."

"More changes," Mirella said. "This is a whole new person we got here. No boat, no Finch, who knows what else is all of a sudden no."

"So she is," I said. "Different. Which we also knew. The question is, do we know anything new?"

"Maybe not," Mirella said.

"But maybe we do," I said. "I wonder how busy that schedule really is."

"You think she was pushing you not to go to Amy-Robsart direct? Like maybe you saw her once, once is enough? More, you might start to wonder?"

"Pushing just a little," I said. "How can we check on the schedule—quietly?"

"Sten Rann," she said at once. "He will have to keep it quiet, and that works for him. Talking to us, and not telling Security, will be a pleasure."

So I checked with Sten Rann, and found that Amy-Robsart's schedule was a long way from crowded, which was not massively surprising.

And next morning I went out into the Palace Garden. I thought I'd be looking for traces, just in case there still were some. I looked, while chatting, but nothing turned up. I found something else, though, and almost at once.

I had just a little trouble getting into the Garden. That was the something else, and its name was Godney Thrall.

Thrall was a little, nervous-looking man wearing a light-blue jumper and, believe it or not, a topee. I think it's called a topee—a solar topee (because it keeps the sun off your head): anyhow, a small pile of fake hair on top of his head. I've seen them in museums, but never on a living human, and they look even worse than you think they ought to. Was there some superstition, back before the Clean Slate War, about hairless people being unlucky? Or a fear of scalp sunburn?

Anyhow, he spotted me coming in through the West Palace entrance—I'd got that far courtesy Sten Rann, just being a tourist—and moved up fast to block me.

"You," he said.

I looked at him. It was a lovely morning, bright and shining. "Me," I said.

"What are you doing here?"

I grinned. "I'm standing here," I said. "Talking to you. Waiting to walk out and look at the flowers."

"Why?"

"Because," I said patiently, "you stopped me."

He gave me a grim look. He had a pretty good grim look, for a man with a solar topee and thin eyebrows. "Don't be funny," he said. "Why are you coming into the Garden?"

"I'm a tourist," I said. "An invited kind of tourist. My name's Gerald Knave. Who the Hell are you?"

"Godney Thrall," he said. "Security." He reached up and straightened the topee. The improvement wasn't noticeable.

"Oh," I said. "You're the one who left Amy-Robsart alone when your shift ended."

This time it was a piercing glance. He wasn't as good with piercing glances. "Who told you that?"

"Everybody," I said. "My God, what a thing to do."

"Look," he said. "That is not your business, Bud. Your business is going away from here. We don't need interruptions. Disturbances."

And a clear, quiet voice said: "Godney? Who's that, Godney?"

"Me," I said before Thrall could open his mouth. "Gerald Knave, Ms. Berringer. We've met."

"Oh," she said. "Yes. Tocks. It *is* Tocks, isn't it?" The uncertainty gave me a small, sudden chill.

Thrall was looking from me to the Garden and back again.

The Garden was thick enough and tall enough where we were so I couldn't make out Amy-Robsart until she came down a path, smiling gently. She had a small, overly calm smile.

"Among other things," I said. "I didn't know you'd be here."

She nodded, walking up to us. Amy-Robsart was a medium-tall girl with long, almost-straight light-blonde hair, a serious, still face and a slim, attractive figure. A rosebud, of a particularly quiet and high-society kind. "Oh, I spend a lot of time here," she said. "It's so—" and she stopped. A long, long second went by while she hunted—not for the right word, I had a feeling, but for the right *reason*. "Peaceful," she said. "That's it, peaceful."

Thrall said: "Ms. Berringer, you know this man?"

"He's Gerald Knave," she said. "He knows about—about Tocks." Then, to me: "It is Tocks, isn't it?" And a small animal came yapping out of the flower-beds.

It was a dog of some kind. I am not checked out on small dogs, but this one looked to be one of the wire-haired breeds, terrors or terriers. It was making the Hell of a racket for its size, and I half expected Godney Thrall to snap to the right stance, and shoot the thing dead. But Thrall remained quiet, and Amy-Robsart picked up the dog when it got near her.

"Hello, Drone," she said, and the dog relaxed all over at once, lying in her arms like a corpse for a few seconds and then reviving enough to try licking her face. She turned to me. "This is Drone," she said. "He's been with me for a long while—a year or two." She still sounded vague, but the dog—a sort of light brown with white spots on it in no pattern I could analyze— seemed to focus her a little.

"Nice to meet you," I told the dog, and then, to Amy-Robsart: "Right, Tocks. I told your maid—"

"Oh yes, the gift," she said, petting the dog. "Coffee. Yes. Sunny did tell me, and I'm sure it'll be wonderful, but we do have to wait. Sunny says so."

Thrall cut in: "Sunny does know best."

"Of course she does," Amy-Robsart said gently. "I know she does. Always."

Thrall turned to me. Grimly. "Well, all right, Knave," he said. "Just watch yourself." He backed away down the path and vanished in a clutter of underbrush.

I was nodding. So was the damn dog, hypnotized by petting. "Why do we have to wait?" I said casually. "I mean, why does Sunny say we have to wait."

She gave me that little calm smile again. "Oh," she said, "I don't really know. I didn't ask. Isn't that the silliest thing?"

What the Hell was going on here? I said: "I hope you enjoyed your sail the other day."

"Oh yes," she said. "I don't think I'll go sailing again for a while, but it was fun. Oh yes. Catamaran."

We talked for a few more minutes—if that's what you want to call what we did. I had one eye and half my mind on the garden, as we wandered, and saw nothing helpful. Then I went away. Fast.

ELEVEN

"Programmed," Mirella said.

I nodded. It was lunch-time, and we were comparing notes back in my rooms. Lunch was thick liverwurst sandwiches on rye bread from a local bakery—I'd been a little too preoccupied to try baking, which is an arcane damn art anyhow—and jugs of iced coffee, sugar and good cream. I took a bite and nodded, and when I had it swallowed I said: "That's how she acted. Not as if she'd had a shock. As if she were acting—as if she were a Totum programmed for speech, and had got pretty good at it. Drone— the dog—brought her out of it, but not very far.'"

"You know," Mirella said, when she'd done some chewing and swallowing herself, "one of these days I am starting a diet again." I looked at her. "Not for looks," she said. "Not even for health, maybe real thin people live longer but maybe it just seems longer. But for the fight. People need something to fight with, so it shouldn't be other people."

"Your call," I said. "But—well, look: if the damn kid's been programmed—who programmed her?"

"Or what," Mirella said. She took in some iced coffee. "Trauma can maybe give you a new program."

"Not like this," I said. "Trauma programs are—fragmented. Bits and pieces. If that happens, what you get is what looks like Scrambled Person. This isn't scrambled, it's one consistent, calm person."

"She was always calm," Mirella said. "The quiet one."

I finished the sandwich. "There are six thousand different kinds of calm people. She was one kind. Nice, self-effacing, quiet. Now she's another kind—polite, a little slow, repetitive— programmed."

"So somebody got a new type out of stock and put her in it, like a tight dress," Mirella said. I nodded—and then I stared at her.

"That," I said, "is an idea. A distinct idea. It explains what's happened—all of what's happened."

"A substitute Amy-Robsart?" she said. "A ringer? Look, that kind of thing is for stories. The Prince and the Puppy, whatever it was. Real life, what happens is there are too many details."

"Sure," I said. "A ringer slides in—let's give her plastic surgery, let's give her new fingerprints, new retina prints, name it—she has nineteen years of memories to soak up first. And absolutely no way of telling which ones she's going to need in the next ten minutes. Anybody can get up the big picture, and some of the important details—but here comes somebody who was a friend back when you were both seven years old—not your best friend even then, but not a stranger—who just happens to be on vacation and visiting Columbus. No way you can do the job, and no way anybody could figure to do it; the ones who try are almost always just a little nuts to begin with. Amy-Robsart the Pretender: it won't work."

Mirella nodded. "Obvious, okay," she said. "So how is it an idea, Jerry?"

"Because maybe it isn't a ringer," I said. "Maybe it's the original—almost."

She sighed. Theatrically. "Okay," she said. "I'll bite. How almost?"

"Two ways," I said. "One: she's had her brain run through a good washer. It can be done—I could change a tiger into a pretty fair rabbit if I had enough time and good enough communication."

"Not inside of a day you couldn't," she said. "How long was she missing? Not long."

"Right," I said. "So we go to Two. Which I like a lot better anyhow: doing effective brainwashing—even if you could do it in a few hours—and leaving *no* physical traces is damn near impossible, in the short run. A bruise, a scar, weight loss—something."

"So two," Mirella said.

"So," I said, "somebody has figured out a way to duplicate people—with revisions."

Her turn to stare. "That," she said after a minute, "is flat impossible."

"Sure," I said. "A clone—let's take the easiest process—is an infant: you'd have to have nineteen years for it to grow up into Amy-Robsart, and then she'd only be Amy-Robsart physically—more or less."

"How more or less?" Mirella said. "A clone is an exact."

"In nineteen years," I said, "things happen. Maybe Amy-Robsart broke her arm once, and the clone, in *its* nineteen years, didn't. Maybe Amy-Robsart never got some childhood disease or other, and the clone did. Maybe anything. And it doesn't matter—nobody had nineteen years to wait while the clone grew up; the damn kid was herself last week."

"So it couldn't happen." she said.

"Maybe," I said, "just maybe, it could. It's not likely—but anything else is impossible."

"Look at it," she said. "What do they say? Eliminate the impossible, and whatever is left, you are stuck with it."

"Sherlock Holmes," I said.

"Right," she said. "We studied it, back in the police. But everything else is really impossible? Because this is an idea I do not truly want to be stuck with."

I sighed. "She's changed," I said. "She wasn't brainwashed. Short of a magic spell, what else have we got?"

Mirella sighed too. "Me," she said, "I would vote for the magic spell. Then at least you *know* it doesn't make sense. But a nineteen-year-old clone who got born last week—what have we got here, time travel?"

"Traveling through time is one of those things the Ancients talked a lot about," I said. "But it's just words. Traveling through time is like traveling through satisfaction, or color: time is a state, not a road."

"Sure," she said. "That much, we know."

"The Ancients figured out it was a dimension," I said. "One of the four elements: air, water, earth and time. I may have that slightly confused. Height, length, air, water—well, a dimension, anyhow. But calling it a dimension doesn't mean you can travel in it: ordinary atomics needs sixteen dimensions for simple description, but nobody thinks there are sixteen directions to travel in."

"So do we need a lecture on Ancient history?" Mirella said. "Say we get a nineteen-year-old clone somehow or other."

"Guy Finch would know," I said. "He was studying biophysics. Clone states, whatever they are."

"Iowa and Kansas," Mirella said. "Arizona and New Mexico. Who can tell the difference? Clone states."

"Arizona has seaports," I said. "But Guy Finch—"

"Is a young kid," Mirella said. "People say he's a nice, quiet type. Not just Sten Rann—I talked to maybe six people, and most of them know this Guy. He is a pretty good kid, by the ones who know. Just quiet, and nice."

"Maybe he is," I said. "And maybe he's just quiet. We'll try to find out."

"So anyhow," Mirella said, "we got a nineteen-year-old clone. Only this one has changes. You got to figure, not changes by accident: so who can do such a thing? Edit people?"

"Damned if I know," I said. "But—you take a photo, 3D or even 2D. You copy it. You can make changes as you copy—dodge, shadow, highlight, cut. Airbrush, for God's sake."

"A picture is one thing," she said. "A picture is a dead object. With dead objects you can do a lot. But—somebody got all the way to figuring how to do this with people? *Live* objects?"

"*You* look at it, Mirella," I said. "It's the explanation. She disappears for a day. When she comes back, she's somebody new. Somebody returned a duplicate. A clone—of sorts. Changed for that somebody's purpose."

"Makes sense, that far," she said. "But—cloning with changes. Editing people. That's already something new."

"Maybe," I said. "The clone has different life experiences, it grows up differently—"

"And you can make it into the person you want?" she said. "Even just with ordinary people, who can do that? Not even close: somebody grows up, he is always a surprise. Or she."

"There's more," I said. "This clone has to have Amy-Robsart's memories. It almost *is* that damn impersonation job."

"Which is flat out impossible, we already had that," Mirella said.

"I think there may be a way," I said. "Not the impossible impersonation job. But it will take some thinking about."

Well, I had a fine opportunity for thinking, at that: I went and did the dishes. My Robbies never do that, unless I'm rushed, very lazy or too tired; it's as restful and thought-inducing an activity as crossword puzzles or solitaire, a fine way to busy the mind without actually occupying it.

And my mind had quite a lot, all of a sudden, to occupy it. A small pile of lunch dishes was hardly enough.

TWELVE

Four o'clock. Cocktails with the Finches.

They were, of course, late. Columbus runs that way—except for the Palace, where people do arrive on the damn dot. Mirella had the place nicely set up, and the Robbies had been programmed for basic cocktail duties long ago. My Totum, who had that program built in, with some additions from me, usually takes the door, but politeness requires a human being, so when the chime went off at four-twenty I was there.

"Hello," I said, "and welcome to both of you."

Astarte Finch gave me a smile as thin as an ice slick. "How nice of you," she said. She was, I'd researched and found out, forty-six; she looked to be in her mummified fifties. She came in past me, and Guy followed.

Guy was a lot of person, judging by height, and not all that much, judging by weight. Six-five or six-six, and if he weighed my one-sixty-five he was carrying lead weights in every pocket. He had a shock of golden hair—if you saw it on a female you'd wonder which coiffeur had done so complete and glaring a job—and large, round horn-rims. His long, thin face was tan, and a little freckled.

In one pocket of his jumper was a bulge the size of a book. His hand kept fingering it.

I shut the door, led them into the living room and indicated chairs. I got Guy onto a small sofa, and his mother on a puffy flowered job halfway across the room from him, and dropped into my chair, more or less between them. "Well," I said. "Very nice of you to come and visit."

"Oh," Astarte Finch said, "I've been wanting to talk to you, ever since we met."

"At the dinner," I said. "I do remember—but we got interrupted." I gave her the pleasantest smile I own. "You were talking about marriage, as I remember."

And Mirella came in, behind my Totum with a trayful. I'd done my basic research, of course.

Guy Finch took a plain soda in a goblet, as expected. The other drinks on the tray were all the same preSpace cocktail, just coming back into fashion—Dockerys. I'd even got real wood

slivers to stick into them, though I won't swear they were au-
thentic hickories—let alone Dockery hickories—and though
the ancients served the things in Dockery goblets, modern Columbus went in for tall glasses. It made for the Hell of a power-
ful drink, and the Totum presented the tray so Astarte had one
obvious choice. She took it, leaving Mirella and me with the
weaker versions.

"Just lovely," she said to me, with a smile one sip of her
drink had made considerably warmer. She turned the smile on
Mirella. "I'm so happy to meet you at last, Ms.—oh, it's *Mrs.*
Puffer, isn't it?"

"It's Mrs. Knave, thanks," Mirella said. "Nice to meet you,
too, Ms. Finch."

"Oh, Astarte," she said. "Please, you must make it Astarte."

Guy was working away slowly at his plain soda, not looking
at anybody. "Very interesting dinner," I said to Astarte,
"though I did regret not being able to continue our talk. Too bad
Ms. Berringer didn't show."

"Ah well," she said, and inhaled the rest of her Dockery.
"These young folk—they have no *idea* of social obligation. Why,
my Guy will run off to his books and things rather than attend
even the most important functions."

Guy looked up, gave everybody a smile a tenth of a second
long, and went back to wherever it was he was living.

"Well," I said, "she does seem to have got the idea now. I
was talking to her yesterday, and she said—"

"Oh, you spoke with little Amy-Robsart?" Astarte said. Her
eyes were a bit wider. "My goodness, how is the dear child?"

The name had set off a program in Guy's head, and suddenly he was looking at me. When he focused, he had eyes that
saw you right down to the bones. "She seems—well, a bit troubled," I said. "I wonder if anything happened to her while she
was off sailing."

"Oh, surely not," Astarte said. "If that were so, she'd have
seen doctors, don't you think? Or at least someone—and I do
know she hasn't, not anyone of that sort. I mean, the dear Emperor's *extremely* careful of his youngest—my goodness, if the
dear girl so much as coughed he'd have specialists running in
from who knows where." She trilled a little laugh. It wasn't as
good as Mirella's is, though it was every bit as fake.

"Possibly," I said. Guy was watching me as if I'd grown five eyes, a trunk and a threatening expression. "But it did seem to me she'd had some kind of a shock. She wasn't quite herself, somehow."

"Young people," Astarte said vaguely. "They do have moods." She looked around a little, and I pushed the button at the outside of my chair-arm. A Robbie scooted over with a Dockery on a tray. "Ah," Astarte said. "How kind." She put half of it down. "You do have lovely service," she said, and smiled at me, or at the retreating Robbie. Or, of course, at the remaining half-Dockery.

"All in the programming," I said. "Tell me—"

"A shock?" Guy said. He put his goblet on the nearby small table and leaned forward at me. Behind his horn-rims his yellow eyes were large and focused. "What sort of shock?"

I shrugged. "Probably nothing," I said. "Perhaps she'd just had a little too much sun at the moment—we met out in the Garden."

"My goodness," Astarte said. "That's where she—" She stopped for a second. "That's where she left her attendant. According to the stories."

"So it is," I said.

"Too much sun," Guy said. "How did she act? I mean, was she vague or something? Unsteady on her feet? Look, if there's anything wrong—"

"Now, Guy dear," Astarte said. "It's nothing. Probably nothing. You heard Mr. Knave say so."

He swung his head around to stare at her. "Mother, let me find *out* what it is," he said. "Please."

"But you're cross-questioning this nice Mr. Knave, and he—"

"Perfectly all right," I said. "We'll cross-question each other." I gave Guy a casual smile. "It wasn't anything that serious," I said. "She seemed to be a little careless about a few small facts. Probably perfectly normal—after all, I don't know her all that well."

"Careless how?" Just the facts, Momma—that was the tone, if you'll forgive the Classical allusion.

"Nothing, really," I said. "She hasn't any real reason to remember things about me, after all. Just because she's interested in Tocks, and I've met some—"

"Tocks," Astarte said. "They're some sort of race, aren't they? Such interesting people, I understand."

"She likes Tocks," Guy said. "She hopes—some day, she'll be able to get off Earth and meet one. Some day. It'll happen." He sounded determined, and for that second there was something new in his voice. "They don't travel, you know. Planet-bound."

No Tock has ever left Haven IV, and as far as anybody can predict none ever will. They have the technology, and God knows they have the brains, but they're glued to the place by whatever set of motives it is Tocks own. "Well, unpleasant though it is to mention it," I said, "her father won't be Emperor forever. And then she'll be able to travel."

"We had plans to go to—" Guy said, and stopped. The new tone had vanished. "She certainly will," he said, with not too much of a pause.

Astarte was holding an empty glass again. "There, you see?" she said "The dear little girl's perfectly fine, Guy. So you don't have to worry. So sweet of you, really, to worry so over the Emperor's relations."

I pressed the button again, and a Robbie came scooting over with a Dockery. Astarte either had the Hell of a metabolism, or the Hell of a lot of practice.

Mirella said, not too suddenly: "Guy, what is it you're studying? I mean, I hear a lot about clones, but what's a clone state? The state a clone gets into when it looks maybe in a mirror?" Good girl. Change things around, and see how they're going to look when another angle comes up. Astarte said:

"Oh, that's all *technical*. You know, such dry, dry things. We needn't talk about that." Slowing down a little, she inhaled only about a third of the latest big glassful of Dockery.

"No," I said. "I'm interested, too. We can never know too much about what makes the worlds tick, don't you think so?" And, to Guy: "Clone states?"

He was in his element, or one of them—the lecture-hall. "Let's begin at the beginning," he said. "When you clone a plant, you get an exact copy."

"When you clone anything you get an exact copy," Mirella said. "This we all know."

"In fact," Guy said, "we don't. Because it isn't so."

THIRTEEN

Astarte said: "So confusing," just as Mirella said: "So how come not?"

Guy ignored his mother, who didn't seem at all miffed; she went back, a bit dreamily, to her drink. "A plant," he said, "has little or nothing in the way of a nervous system."

Mirella shook her head. "Plants can be very weird," she said. "Some of them even eat people. Earth plants, originally from Venus, right? Flytraps, they call them."

Guy looked at her, resignedly. "The Venus's flytrap eats small insects," he said. "It is purely an Earth plant—the origin of the name, I'm afraid, I don't know."

"Big disappointment," Mirella said "Here I was looking to see one while we are on planet. A plant zoo, some kind. See how they feed the things—like sacrificing virgins in the *real* old days."

"Charming," Astarte said, from far, far away.

"There exists a reflex system in certain plants," Guy said. "In many plants, to some degree: phototropism provides another example. But in the sense required, only animal life has a nervous system—and we have to consider, essentially, only mammals—among Earth forms. Other forms of life present other questions—which we'll have to deal with, some day. But for the present . . ."

He considered for a second or so, and Astarte said: "My goodness, what a topic for cocktail conversation."

"Why not?" Mirella said, thank God. "Science advances. Somebody finds a new trick with clone states might even get to be famous. Then everybody would be talking about it—we're just ahead of the pack, right?"

Astarte smiled, looked thoughtful and then smiled more brightly. She opened her mouth to say something or other, probably agreement, but Guy was going on.

"In a sufficiently complex nervous system—that of a cat, for instance, or certain dogs, or of course simians or humans—duplication in the adult clone is not quite exact."

A wildly old-fashioned light bulb was about to go off over my head, but I restrained it. "There are differences?" I said.

He nodded, lost in the lecture hall. "Small, and unpredictable," he said. "The state of the nervous system at a given time is dependent on factors cloning—or, more properly, mirroring, duplication of an existent organism—ordinarily doesn't deal with. The electrochemical field surrounding the more complex brain functions isn't duplicated in the clone; the 'personality' of the clone, so to speak, is different. The differences may not exist in a given case; but they may, and we cannot predict. A human duplicate, for instance, might be—"

I blinked. "Slowed down, maybe?" I said. "Forgetful, odd?"

"Not at all," he said. "Simply different—as any two people are different. We are speaking now not only of cloning at the beginnings of life, but of theoretical duplication beyond it. Personality may be resident in the electronic microstates—there are unpredictable uncertainties involved. But even a clone, somehow given the same experiences and life pattern as its original, will not develop into a duplicate of the original. There are differences, unmistakable and unpredictable."

"Heisenberg," I said, and Astarte said, so help me:

"Lovely place, full of old castles."

"Heisenberg," Guy said. "Uncertainty. Quite right. There is no way to predict what that 'personality' would be, not in advance. We only know that clones show distinct and individual patterning at the electrochemical-field level—and we know this is not an environmental effect; it's built in from birth, so to speak. At a level we cannot yet reach or control—if it is ever reachable."

"It sounds," Mirella said, "like a total mystery. A kind of lab thing. Who can figure what is the use?"

"Oh," Guy said, "at the moment we don't know much. But we will. And there'll be a thousand uses for it, when we understand it a little better."

My head was making connections with blinding speed. "I can see that," I said casually. "I think. What work are *you* doing with it?"

"Theoretical, mostly," he said. "The maths—field strengths related to the complexity of the nervous system—more exactly, the brain functions—involved. I hope to get into the lab work, but the maths are my strength, and that's where I seem to be useful."

"Oh, *useful*," Astarte said, and trilled her little laugh again. "Really, Guy."

"I wonder if the Tocks know anything about this stuff," Mirella said. Bless her devious heart. "Amy-Robsart might know."

"She understands a lot about it," Guy said earnestly. "She does want to listen—*she* sees the importance." He paused. In a much lower voice he added: "Or she did, at any rate. She did."

The expression in his voice—and on his face—would have cued anyone but Astarte to the knowledge that Guy was harboring a Passion, and a Passion in difficulties. But Astarte was finishing off her Dockery at the time. I cued a Robbie.

"Thank you *so* much," she said, though whether to me or the Robbie I don't know. "Young people and their hobbies," she added vaguely, and belched.

"Mother," Guy said tensely, "it's not a *hobby*. This work—"

"Yes, dear," she said, and took a long swallow.

"I can see it fascinates you," I said. "You're a lucky fellow. Enjoying the work you do is a great gift."

"It's important work," he said. And Astarte said:

"But tell us about *your* work, Mr. Knave. I'm sure it's fascinating. A Survivor. My goodness."

"Knave, Mother," Guy said. "He prefers Knave."

Her head turned toward him. Just a little slowly and carefully. "That's what I said, dear," she told him. "Knave. Mr. Knave. That's his *name*, dear."

"So it is," I said cheerfully. And I spun a few yarns for her. Nothing complex, nothing that required full use of the mind. Mirella chipped in a word or two as needed, and Guy subsided slowly back to his own world.

And the chime went off, and my Totum wheeled to the door—cocktail politeness was needed for Astarte Finch, but why overdo the damn thing?—and in a minute or so Claude Deke was being introduced to everybody.

I'd thought of him as tall and thin, but Guy was a couple of inches higher. They did seem to weigh about the same. Deke got himself into a good chair, a Robbie came around with a Dockery (Astarte was still working on her latest, with slow dedication), and he took out a small box of official-looking tapes, and combed a freckled hand through his bright red hair. "I thought we were going to discuss things," he said.

"We are," I said. "Holly. This strange new place you're sending somebody out to. We've been talking biophysics; it's time for a little planetology."

"Strange new place?" Mirella said, on cue.

He glared at her. "This isn't public information yet, Ms. Knave."

"Mrs.," Mirella said. Firmly. "Look: I am not a Ms., because everybody is a Ms., it's not useful. No meaning to it."

"She's a Mistress," Astarte said helpfully.

"Mrs.," Mirella said. She gave Deke a pretty good return glare. "Mrs. means something," she said. "It says—he is coming back. He goes out to work, he goes out to play, *and he comes back*. Jerry—he has nothing to do that, which is a shame."

"But—" Deke said.

"He ought to have something, says *I* will come back," Mirella said. "Not so he will know it. That, we got: he knows, and I know. That is solid. But—" She stuck a finger at him. "So he has something he can take out and look at, he gets worried. Because that happens: people worry, even when they know."

It was all true, and it was all sense. And it deflected Deke's anger and puzzlement beautifully. I have never been a team player, and the reason is, I never found a team I could trust as much as I trust me—which is not all that far.

I have one now.

There was a little silence. Then Deke said: "Mrs. Knave. Sorry." And Astarte trilled her little laugh. And Mirella said: "Holly? I mean, you're with friends, right? This is not going to the newsreaders, it is not headed for a comm net. Forget the tapes: talk. Holly?"

He nodded. "Holly," he said. "Sun a G6. That's unusual, but orbital distance is about three times Earth Standard, and temp range is all right. Radiation pattern isn't at all bad, surprisingly, and looks good for the next million, maybe. Maybe more."

He'd fallen into lingo, of course. Guy had no more trouble following him than I did, and Mirella was right with us. Astarte was nodding dreamily, perfectly content with the simple, undemanding sound of voices.

"Orbital distance?" I said. "That's the oddity?"

He shook his had and grinned at me. "It's not alone in its orbit," he said. Guy blinked behind those horn-rims.

"Trojan planets?" he said, just before I could. Deke shook his head again.

"Cometary, we thought," he said. "Actually, asteroidal. The sun—the discoverer called it Stoplight, of all the damn names—owns five planets, three small inner ones too hot and too barren to be possibles, and two big outer jobs, away the Hell out. And an asteroid belt."

I stared. "My God," I said.

"Right," he said, and grinned. "One of those asteroids is about the size of—oh, Mercury. Or Haven IV. It's part of a small subsystem—the effect is, it's got nine moons. The balance among the moons helps keep a nice atmosphere for the big asteroid."

"Collisions," I said.

"It's not that thick an asteroid belt," he said. "And the thing looks stable. The subsystem is, for sure—and the whole damn belt's been run through every computer check we can think of. There might be a collision in the belt—might hit Holly. That's the big asteroid—the planet. Might be one here, too, something might hit Earth—comets and asteroids have come damn close. But the might-be's about the same, both cases."

"I will be damned," I said. Astarte hadn't reacted to the notion that something might hit the Earth. Her Dockery was very nearly gone. She was moving the glass in the air, gently, back and forth. "A habitable asteroid," I said. "Not for a dome or a group. Not for a resource mining operation. A world."

"It's a once," Deke said. "Stable orbits, just far enough out, just big enough, the subsystem—nothing like it anywhere. It needs a good Survivor to check it out."

"I can see that," I said. "A lot of questions. Life on Holly?"

"Vegetation," he said. "Animal—maybe. Intelligent—no. Not as far as the drone ships can tell us. Signatures look compatible. It looks very good, Knave."

I said it again: "I will be damned."

"We'll probably send Bruno Carr," he said. "Since you're on leave."

I nodded. Carr would gum it up. He usually did. But how could I argue?

Mirella said: "Stoplight I can see. Love it, no, but I can see it. But why Holly?"

"We thought of it as cometary at first," he said. "Before the plots came in."

"So?"

"Holly," he said. "After Holly's Comet."

It was a temptation. It was the Hell of a temptation.

Holly—a truly unusual world. A year answering questions, living alone on a new planet, a planet that was part of an asteroid belt around a G6 . . .

Luckily, I didn't have to resist it for long. The next morning, I got supplied with a brand-new motive for digging into the travails of Amy-Robsart Berringer.

I have never come any closer to getting killed. If Mirella hadn't been a Lance-Corporal of police, once upon a time, I might be lying somewhere cool and dark right now, with a tag tied to my toe.

And a little sign on my nose, visible to the Recording Angel, that said: "Careless. Just once."

FOURTEEN

Glenn Hanford wasn't that lucky.

Well—we'd gone, that morning, and while mulling the facts we now had, to watch the Changing of the Guard.

The Columbus Palace Guard is Changed every three months, so we were a) lucky to be there when it happened, and b) stuck at the inner edge, more or less, of one of those crowds you read about—"Six Crushed To Death As Thousands Press Forward". People come to see the ceremony from all over the damn planet. We were near the front because I am a Survivor, and Mirella has been a police Lance-Corporal, and we know tricks. We didn't get crushed to death because nobody did; it wasn't quite that awful, though it sure as Hell felt even worse.

There *are* people—not a lot—who go out of their way to avoid the standard tourist attractions, anywhere. Put them on Kingsley and they'll shut their eyes if they have to pass the Tower of Palaces; put them on Earth and they'll damn well fall into the Grand Canyon rather than look at it. This is silly: tourist attractions are what they are because they're interesting. If they weren't, what tourists would they attract?

The Changing of the Guard is fascinating, and not only for mechanicians. For them, it's a must—no Robbies so complex, and no Totum group so large, exists anywhere, outside the factory groupings in Mars Dome. And the Mars Dome mechs are simple and specialized, more or less.

The Palace Guard consists of the only talking Robbies I've ever heard of. Totums can talk, if suitably programmed; Robbies just don't have the spare capacity. But the Guard talks—and marches, bows, smiles and watches. Especially watches; they *are* a Guard, and a damn good one. Assassination is still a useful political tool here and there—but not, not ever, in Columbus. The Robbies are fast, and the Totums, who each accept data from small groups of Robbies, and share it, in doing the mapping, judging and decision-making, are even faster.

A Change every eight months would be satisfactory, mechanicians have told me. But it's an example—like the talking Robbies—of what the Ancients called, I think, Conspicuous Conception: showy money-spending on unnecessary items. You spend the cash just because you *can* spend the cash, and damn well want people to know you can.

Most parts that run down are Changed. Power packs (because, though atomic, they're short-life radioactives—shielded, naturally—for weight-saving), speech assemblies (because Robbies can't speak—but these do), most movable joints, and wheels. And it's all ceremonial: a Changing team—still more Robbies—comes out with tools and gear, and a small army of humans and Totums goes to work on one Robbie at a time.

Those speech assemblies: what they are is recognition circuits, plus a selection of small, randomized tape replies. If you say the right phrase to a Guard, he'll reply with one of four sentences; say another key phrase and one of another four sentences will pop out. It impresses Hell out of tourists.

It impresses Hell out of me, too—those assemblies are not nanobuilt, they're sizable. That some bright engineer managed to fit the things into Robbies, without injuring speed of response for important circuitry—like watching, motion and, if necessary, using blast (yes, it has happened)—is a small and showy miracle.

So there we were, near the front of a pushing, gawking, murmuring crowd, using hands, feet, elbows and wits to keep upright and more or less positioned to see—while the team went to work on its second Robbie of the morning. I wanted to see a little more of the assembly package than I'd been able to with the first—bad angle—and I shifted to my left just before—a tenth of a second before—somebody behind me went Yow.

It wasn't really Yow—it wasn't a spellable sound. I turned around in a tearing hurry, caught some craning woman on the nose with a wrist as I stopped, and headed toward the noise. Mirella wasn't behind me, she was ahead of me.

She has, like most women, fewer restraints about damaging women than I do. It gave her a small edge. The crowd had begun to react, in the vicinity of the sound—people were shoving away from a center, clearing space, and the noise level had risen all at once, and stayed high. Down there, in the middle of a circle of tourists, was somebody who'd been hurt. Badly. The sound had given me that.

And, as I moved, Mirella backed into me, and shoved me off-balance.

There was a sound like *spung*, barely audible over the sudden racket of the crowd. Where I'd been, a large object flew by, knocked off the hat of a small woman, destroying it, and disappeared into the distance.

We got to the cleared space fast. There was a man on the ground in a bright-yellow jumper, very expensive for looks. He had a four-inch assembly bolt for a moving joint—knee, I thought—sticking out of the front of his head: two inches of it were visible.

He'd died instantly, of course. The bolt was about half an inch in diameter. He'd made one sound as the thing went in—as it began to go in—and before he'd finished making it he'd been dead. His name, we found out later, was Glenn Hanford, but that doesn't really matter—except, of course, to Glenn Hanford and any related Hanfords in Taipei, which is where he'd come from to gawk.

There was the Hell of a lot of noise. Somebody, just audible through it, said the expected sentence: "Get a doctor!" Somebody else—far away, maybe eight feet through solidly packed people—said, loudly and determinedly: "I'm a surgeon, let me through."

I stepped into the clear space, standing about four inches from the body. Mirella came around to its other side. People were shoving and screaming all around us.

"He's dead," I said. "We're going to want your names." I gave the crowd one fast, unpleasant look. I didn't specify the We. Mirella said:

"There are going to be some questions asked."

We sounded official, and we sounded threatening as Hell. Noise level dropped, raggedly and fast. The crowd wavered, and muttered, and began to dissolve. A man in his sixties, with sparse grey hair and a grim expression, came panting and pushing through to us.

"Out of the way," he said. In bursts, between pants. "I'm a surgeon."

I said: "He's dead. And he shouldn't be touched."

He snapped at me: "I'll decide if he's dead," and leaned past me. I let him by; he took one long look, laid a couple of fingers against the body's throat, waited and stood up again. "This man's dead," he said, just as if it were news.

I looked across the body, at Mirella, and nodded. Then I told the doctor: "Stay right here. Somebody will be along in less than two minutes." It was a safe bet; the first stir of police, team members, and every damn body else had hit the edge of the crowd and was working in as the crowd faded.

Mirella and I vanished. Fast.

FIFTEEN

My place wasn't far. We got there without any fuss. On the way I said: "Thanks," and Mirella said:

"So a second shot looked likely. Never follow a predictable path."

"Damn it, I was hurried," I said.

"And careless," she said, and I didn't argue it. We got home without further chatter.

I shut the door and Mirella said:

"Okay, eliminate the once in a million. Accident."

I shrugged and sat down. "You can't eliminate it," I said. "Accidents happen. One-in-a-million shots happen, too—one time in every million, give or take. You can't rule them out. But you can damn well manage not to believe in them. Especially when they happen twice."

"Who was he?" she said.

"I didn't check papers. Tourist—nice clothes, mid-crowd, no apparent weaponry."

"Tucked away somewhere?"

"Knife in a trouser-leg, maybe. Small holdout gun any-where. Not more. Anybody official would have had more—I'd have seen signs of some of it. So would you. Tourist."

"Oh God," Mirella said. "You did the angle on the first shot?"

I grinned at her. "I shifted a little just as the thing went by. I might have heard it if the crowd had shut up. From the disas-sembled Robbie—part-disassembled—to me to the tourist was a nice straight line. If I hadn't shifted, the tourist would be snapping 3D shots of my body this minute. And if you hadn't shoved me—"

Mirella spread her hands. "Oh God," she said again. "We have got ourselves into something."

"No," I said. "We did that days ago. Now somebody else has taken a chair. Somebody I've met, or not met yet. If not—I will."

"You?" Mirella said. "Me. I'm insulted. Standing right there, and did *I* get shot at? You, twice. Me, nothing. Somebody is underestimating."

"You might have been next," I said comfortingly, "in the milling around. But he missed with the first shot, took a fast second, and quit. Whatever he had for a third shot, if anything, he decided to save it."

"When we find him," she said, "I could ask him. Hard." She nodded. "Just by the way, why 'he'?"

I shrugged. "Why not? He, she or it. At the moment, all we know is—somebody connected with the Palace."

"With Palace Security," she said. "Somebody had to know to gimmick a Robbie—disassembled, all you'd need would be one circuit order—remoted to the joint at one special second. Not a part of the Changing team."

"No," I said. "They work together—somebody would've been noticed keying the shots."

"But nearby," she said.

"Right," I said. "Had to be there to see me, in the crowd. He had to know just where I was and when. He had to recover and take his second shot, too."

"Or in the Palace, with binocs, something," she said. "Better angle view from there. Key the Robbie by remote: unlock and blast, the way you do for a stuck bolt. Had to be able to see you, a clear line and the Robbie, for bolt angle on release." She thought for a second. "Any window facing," she said. "Not binocs—strap-on lenses. Get maybe ten-times magnification, maybe fifteen, good enough. Leave hands free for keying the remote, whatever it was."

I nodded. "Palace Security, or Palace mechanician," I said. "Either way. Or even somebody around the Palace who's read up on the Changing—not tough."

"And had access to the Robbie, to plant the keying circuit," she said. "If that can get found—"

"No chance," I said. "Stick-on circuitry, six molecules thick, on the damn leg, close to the bolt. Vaporized with the key command. Same for the second, whatever it was—my guess is the other knee bolt, and who cares? Why take chances?"

Mirella grinned at me. "So he might be careless too," she said. "Hoping is illegal?"

I grinned back. "One more thing," I said. "The window. The room it's in had to be deserted—and dependably deserted. Somebody with strap-on lenses, holding a remote, watching the first shot and keying a second—people might notice."

She nodded. "Good point," she said. "So where do we start?"

*　　*　　*

Ringing in the local police was out. There was no way I could see to do that without somebody getting Palace Security involved—and Palace Security might already be involved—on the wrong side.

No, this was going to be our job.

"Connected to Amy-Robsart?" Mirella said. "Because that does not have to be so."

"Hell of a coincidence if it isn't," I said. "It's possible that somebody in Columbus hates me for other reasons. I've been providing reasons, off and on, for years. But—this is somebody *connected with the Palace* who hates me."

"Even so—"

"And who didn't take a much better shot at me, the night of the dinner," I went on. "Who either wasn't there then, or couldn't arrange a nice remote like today—or didn't have a motive to try shoving a bolt through my skull then. I hadn't started looking at Amy-Robsart back then."

"When you're right," Mirella said, "you're right. And one more thing—"

"I know," I said. Mirella nodded.

"Had to know you were there," she said. "Had to know you'd be there."

"Not quite," I said. "One bolt from one Robbie—aimed just right. The second comes with the package—an in-case extra. Even if the disassemblies are placed the same way, every Changing—I doubt they're that precise. Nobody could have figured I'd be right there, right then, at a good angle for a shot. Not in advance."

She shook her head. "You're telling me this was accident," she said. "Or coincidence. Which I do not believe, and *you* do not believe. This was aimed, and aimed at you. I am still insulted, not at me, but maybe next time, the son of a bitch. Make it daughter of a bitch, take your damn pick."

Mirella never swears. Never. I looked at her. "It's all right," I said. "He missed. Twice. No harm done—though Glenn Hanford would disagree. And the lady with the hat might have a small complaint."

"No," she said. "I know he missed. It's done, it's over. But while I was talking, also I was thinking. Not accident, not coincidence."

"I thought you'd see it," I said. She nodded. Grimly. Damn grimly.

"Whoever—" she gestured with one abrupt hand—"whoever, he had this set up. In case, not the second shot but both shots. A good bet you'd be there, a good bet you'd get front. Maybe when he sees you he gets the Robbie arranged for angle, to get disassembled. If the bet comes off, he keys his remote. Bam."

"Right," I said. "And—"

"And if he makes one good bet," she said, "he makes sixty good bets. He's got other stuff set up—who knows where, who knows what?"

I grinned at her. "It's a mine field," I said. She said:

"Your what?" Then she nodded. "Oh. Right. Buried explosive. A mine. I heard about it—old-time stuff, mostly. A field full of mines." The gesture again, a hard jerk of one hand and arm. "The whole city is a field of mines for you," she said.

"For us," I told her. "Let's share."

"Okay." A sigh—not theatrical, just a sigh. "We are going to have to be careful," she said. "We are going to have to watch everything."

I nodded. "So what else is new?"

"More than usual," she said.

"All right," I said. "We'll be careful as all Hell. That's been good before, it'll be good now."

"So," Mirella said. "I try to watch you, you try to watch me. I also try not to worry. Jerry, this is all of a sudden a lot of trying."

"Also," I said, "we try to find this son of a bitch. Daughter. I'm not really fond of getting shot at."

That brought a grin I was happy to see. "You got a place to start?" she said, and we got down to finding one.

SIXTEEN

There was a small barrel of candidates, when we looked at it. Astarte Finch. Horace FoFeality.

"FoFeality knows from machines," Mirella said. "FoFeality is Palace Security. So why not?"

"It might be," I said, "but it doesn't really add up, does it? We've got all these careful plans, and we've got the man who makes them being so very visible?"

"So he's careless," Mirella said. "With FoFeality, this is a surprise?"

"We'll keep him on the list, God knows," I said. "But just one of the crowd, for now. Our Horace likes the shadows too much to put himself in the spotlight like this; it's out of character, I think."

Mirella gestured. "He has a character?" she said. And then: "All right. Okay. Guy Finch."

"For the sake of completeness," I said. "No more than that. You saw him. Hard to believe."

"Hard," she said, "is not impossible."

"Right," I said.

And there were, of course, a few others. Sunny Samuels. Godney Thrall.

And people I hadn't met—yet. Martina Greensinger, who'd been Thrall's relief the day Amy-Robsart had vanished from the Garden, and who'd so conveniently turned up late.

She looked promising. But there wasn't enough data. *Anybody* looked promising. And nobody looked more than promising.

"Amy-Robsart is the youngest," Mirella said. "So maybe one of the other kids is jealous. She gets a lot of attention—the Finch woman said it, Deke said it."

"The Empress is in Djakarta with Roesan," I said. "The two other kids—Antonio, doing some kind of graduate naval work at Cambridge, and Rosella, with her parents."

She shrugged. "Things could be arranged from Djakarta," she said. "Or from Cambridge. From Mars Dome, it comes to that."

"What difference?" I said. "If it's being arranged, there has to be somebody right here to do the work. Grab Amy-Robsart, duplicate-and-edit somehow and return, gimmick a Robbie's knee joints. Find that person, and we can ask some questions, if we have to. It's still the same job: finding somebody right here. Palace connections." I paused. "You've been talking to people," I said. "Who do you know that I don't know?"

"Greensinger is home with a cold," she said. "People here still *get* colds—traditional, maybe. Some housekeeping people, an under-butler—supporting cast, you know? They don't look right for this—good at their jobs, maybe, but their jobs is what they know. Not much outside, and this one took talent."

"Right," I said. "So we pry something loose. First, we go after the mechanicians. Who knows what about what, how set are the Changing routines, all of that."

"Then the room," she said. "The supporting cast will know something, they oversee cleaning, whatever."

"We'll split it," I said. "You take the room—you've talked to some of the people, you're already inside."

"Fine," she said.

"And while we're doing all that," I said, "we try—very hard—to be very careless."

She laughed. "Again?" she said. "Make it easy for him?"

"Pull him into making another try," I said. "Every time he does something, he gives up some facts. Right now, we're in the fact-collecting business."

"So we hope," Mirella said, "his next try isn't maybe a little too good. Fact collecting is fine; damage collecting we do not need to do."

"We'll be nice, obvious targets," I said. "And very safe ones. It helps any target to know he is one."

"Or she," Mirella said. "Maybe this time he tries for me."

But he didn't—or not specifically. The next try was a beaut, and it was aimed at both of us.

We were dealing with somebody who knew Robbies. Or Totums, but that came to the same thing—people who know about atoms know about molecules. Whether our Robbies or the Totum had been gimmicked there was no immediate way to tell—the innards might provide a clue, but that meant stripping the things down and doing a long job of work. I'd do that—

I'd known my mechs for years. But before I started: we were dealing with somebody who knew Robbies.

And just possibly somebody who knew chemistry. Though it hadn't been a very rare poison.

We were also dealing with somebody who wasted no time at all. My God, you'd think—having tried twice and missed—he'd go away till the next day, if only to figure out what his best next move was.

Instead, he gimmicked dinner that night.

We ate in, relaxing and thinking of ways to make targets out of ourselves. Cooking helps me think, anyhow, almost as much as washing dishes does, and I'd found a nice mess of King prawns to batter-fry, with green beans soaked in Madeira and butter, and scalloped potatoes to contrast with the crusty batter-fried prawns. We were both drinking Charlie Brown's Celery Tonic—because the stuff just isn't available off Earth, and there's no taste quite like it.

I'd done the cooking, but that's the fun part, and our Robbie did the serving. Nothing difficult or out of program: he set a table, identified the pots and pans, found plates, dished out and came rolling in with a plate in either hand.

Everything looked fine. But we *were* being careful.

Back in ancient times, rich people—Emperors, Popes, Kennedys—had taste-testers. Possibly test-tasters. If somebody wanted to poison you, he'd get the taste-tester instead, because you waited to begin on your dinner until you were sure the taste-tester wasn't going to curl up and turn blue.

It must have been a very handy set-up, for anybody who wanted to poison a taste-tester (and what the Hell, everybody has enemies)—and, of course, it meant that you ate your meals cold. These days, there's a quicker way, one that doesn't use up taste-testers.

Very few people know about it, and even fewer have the interest or the capacity—just in terms of available equipment—to rig the thing. I'm one of the people who knows about it, and after the Adventure of the Shot Bolts I'd developed the interest in a hurry.

The available equipment, and the knowledge of what to hook into what where, I had stockpiled. I'd had the equipment in a closet for years—because you never do know.

It's a shield field, with a display focus up near the ceiling, six feet above the dining-room table. It's programmed for every ingredient in every dish you're going to put on the table—in this case prawns, batter, butter, salt, pepper, brown sugar, bread crumbs (hard rye), vinegared butter for the frying liquid, green beans, Madeira . . . well, it's a long list, but it doesn't strain the field capacity; you could do a mulligatawny, six pies and a stuffed turkey with trimmings, and the thing would never hiccup.

Oh—the pepper and brown sugar? Small, almost equal amounts. The prawns are soaked in warm water with the pepper and brown sugar before battering. Try it some time. Rub garlic on the hard rye before you crumb it.

When our Robbie put the plates down, the field flashed blue. I'd filled Mirella in on the gimmick, and she said: "It's kidding, right? Fast worker, this one."

"It doesn't kid," I said. She nodded. "Damn it, that came out well, too. Punch up a phone order."

"I was looking forward," she said. "How do we do chem analysis?"

"The field does it," I said. "Has done it, in fact." I looked at the readout, which I'd programmed to print from my Totum, standing nearby. "Potassium cyanide," I said. "Order a couple of pizzas. With everything."

"Cyanide, I am not fond of," Mirella said. "Pizza, not much more."

"We're not going to eat the pizzas," I aid. "But we're damn well going to think ahead. Our fast little Whoever gimmicked the dinner—somehow. He may also have an in-case again—in case the gimmick doesn't work. If I were him, I'd have put a beam tap on the phone—a remote job, no need to come in here to do it—and get to whatever place we ordered from. Maybe bop the delivery person—Columbus is full of human-service joints—and substitute, poisoning the pizza on the way." I shook my head. "Though, damn it, he *did* come in here. Had to."

"Oh," she said. "Right. And while I'm ordering pizza—"

"I'll be down the street finding a public phone, to order a dinner we can probably eat. Any suggestions? And let's be *entirely* safe—write the dinner order down, don't say it. It might be a general tap, not just the phone; but a small written note is something we can shield by hand, and destroy."

Mirella had been looking forward to seafood, but (by return note) I vetoed it—too predictable, and there was no way of telling, until I took the Robbie and Totum apart, whether our little Whoever knew what we'd planned for dinner. We finally settled on a steak house that did take-out, and I left.

Expensive place: delivery was by individual Totum. But that gave us a small additional safety factor: even if our little Whoever managed to bop a Totum, he couldn't make the delivery: it's not really a workable disguise. We left the field on, programming for all the ingredients we knew or could predict in the dinner—and of course the thing flashed blue, and the readout told me there was sea salt on the onion rings, of all the damn things. Sea salt is not poisonous, but onion rings don't need it.

But they were edible, as was everything else. Some day, I'd try the prawns again.

And we now had something more to think about, and to discuss.

"He got to the Robbie, and this time he got to the kitchen," I said. "He had to be here, had to come in here, some time. One question: when?"

"Two questions," Mirella said. "Also how. I have seen your safeties, and I like your safeties. They are very sexy things, though there are other things you got, outclass them for sexy." She gave me a grin. "How is also a big question."

I shook my head. "A lock, even a field lock, even mine—one that can't be gimmicked doesn't exist. And in this case, getting in may have been easy. I'm not the only one who knows the unlock."

She stared. "Me?" she said. "Now wait a minute. Wait one large bright red minute. *Me?* You think *I* let something slip that—"

I had my hand up, with a forkful of steak in it. "For God's sake," I said. "No. Let's try it again." I chewed steak. "We are the only two humans who know the unlock. We are the only two people—intelligent beings of any race—who know it. But there are others."

"Right," she said. "Ghosts." Then she got it. "Sure. The Totum knows it."

"The Totum opens the damn door," I said. "If I'm away he can open it for me, on my ID. And you have to know the unlock to do that."

"Took me a second," Mirella said.

"And if somebody got to the Totum," I said, "somebody who knows something about them—"

"So how—without getting in first? And he gets in first, this Whoever, he can't use the Totum's brain to help, he hasn't got in yet to gimmick the Totum to tell him."

"But the Totum goes *out*," I said. "Not often. In the time we've been here, this trip, twice."

"Tell me," she said. "I didn't file that."

"No reason to remember it," I said. "But I sent him on a shopping trip, the first few days we were here. Three days before the dinner."

"Not that time," Mirella said. "Back then, nobody was aiming for you. Aiming starts after the dinner—when you start poking around about Amy-Robsart. I mean—when we do."

"Right," I said. "And the second time *was* after the dinner. A job lot of files and forms, just tying off loose ends with Colonization. I have better things to do than deliver data files to Colonization by hand, and the sooner they got there the faster we'd tie off the last loose end. So I sent the Totum over with them."

Mirella blinked. She cut a careful piece of steak, chewed it and swallowed it. Then she said: "To Colonization?"

I nodded. "To Claude Deke."

SEVENTEEN

"I do not believe one word," Mirella said. "Not the Claude and not the Deke. I can barely believe the To."

"I'm not fond of it myself," I said. "And of course it doesn't have to be Deke. He gets a look—he gets a lot of looks—but while the Totum was out—"

"Somebody lassoes him," Mirella said, "gimmicks him whatever way he needs, and sends him on his way With a little erase to take care of things, the Totum can never report a thing. By the Totum it never happened."

"Right," I said. "Anybody might have done it—anybody who could have been on a street in Columbus when my Totum wandered by. Which doesn't look like much help." I gave her a grin. "But you're wrong."

She swallowed the last bit of steak, and fished for an onion ring. "Wrong how?" she said. "This Whoever, he grabs—or she grabs, let's keep our minds nice and open—she grabs, she gimmicks, she erases. How wrong?"

"You said, for the Totum it never happened," I said. "For this particular Totum, I will make a nice bet that isn't so."

Mirella returned the grin, with interest. "You put in a backup," she said.

"A backup gets looked for," I said. "It's an extra box, somewhere. Anybody who erases the data will look for a backup, and erase the backup too."

"So?"

I swallowed a couple of potato wedges. "I put in an echo."

Mirella shook her head. "I am a simple barefoot police person," she said. "Technical details lose me very fast. Tell."

"No extra box," I said. "But every event the Totum experiences happens twice for him. The circuitry looks a little scrambled, but it may not be noticeable, if you're not looking for it very specifically. Every echo—the *repeat* of an event—gets stored in the brain."

She stared. "And this fits in a normal Totum shell?" she said. "I know things can get small, but—every event, over maybe years of action, is a lot of event."

"Every seventy-two hours, it washes out," I said. "Not

73

completely—but any event repeated three times or more is wiped, all three, or seven, or whatever. If the Totum oversees serving dinner, it remembers the last two times; if it opens the door, it remembers the last two times. Unique events are stored for good."

"Very," Mirella said, and swallowed Celery Tonic, "handy. And how do we call this echo up, we can see what happened? Because being grabbed on a public street is going to be a unique event."

"I hope so," I said. "We finish dinner, and for a change the Robbie does the dishes. While he's doing that, I ask the Totum. It takes a special sequence to ask him. Then I'll set up for 3D display."

"Great," Mirella said. "The 3D display can be dessert. I'll start a diet, no pie."

"Just by the way," I said, spearing the last potato wedge, "why are Robbies and Totums always he? I mean—our Who-ever might be anybody, and you worry about he-or-she. But Robbies and Totums are always male. Why is that?"

Mirella shrugged. "Obvious," she said. "They're servants. Big, strong fetch-and-carry things." She considered. "Also," she said, "they are not really all that bright."

Forty minutes later—it's a complex sequence, for good reason, and setting up a link with a 3D took a little time—we sat down in the living-room and let the Totum replay its trip out into the big world.

Out the door, down the elevator, through the lobby—I'm all for private houses, if you live in one all the time, but when you go away for a year at a stretch a nice apartment in an apart-ment block, with no outside maintenance to worry about, is a better bet—and out into North Evans Boulevard. The replay has a clock check supered in, lower right front, a little square that told us it was 2:16:32 P. M. local.

North Evans isn't as crowded as some of the other streets near the Palace. The Totum rolled along, passing an occasional pedestrian and tipping its hat politely as it went by—from the neck up it's an ancient British butler, complete with derby or durban or whatever that was—and turned, after two blocks, onto Imperial Way West.

That's a busy enough street to have an auto lane, for Totums and other non-car automatics, as well as a pedestrian lane and a four-lane highway. and the Totum rolled along on it, passing a couple of Robbies but not going at any breakneck burnout speed; it was, after all, just a casual errand. Five blocks of auto lane.

Then a right turn onto Boomerang Street. Columbus was rebuilt, of course, after the Clean Slate War—some while after—and rebuilt again about fifty years ago, and Boomerang's a new street. There was a blockage, some sort of repair going on. Not unusual, and I was more than willing to put it down to coincidence: nobody could have preplanned grabbing my Totum on Boomerang Street at a particular time on a particular day. Hell, I might have decided to lug the files over myself, by car.

But Boomerang Street was the spot. A little over two blocks down from Imperial West, there's a small park, with trees coming right out to the street edge. The auto lane goes outside the trees, and the pedestrian path curves left around a small stand of elms.

The Totum, blocked from the auto lane, veered left and started under the trees. It wasn't a busy moment for the street—I saw one woman walking away from the Totum, ahead of it about thirty feet.

It stopped dead.

Magnetic drop, of course, probably a small field. Somebody came from behind a tree—not looking furtive, just ambling along—and took the Totum's hand. The somebody pushed a switch on a small box in one hand, and the Totum turned, and then went along with its new friend.

The new friend was not really a surprise. He didn't look any more kindly and cheery than he'd looked playing semicomputer billiards at one of his clubs, and he was perfectly recognizable.

Mirella snorted. "I knew it," she said. "He had to be in this someplace, besides just being a bad smell."

"FoFeality," I said. "If you had to hire a mechanician for a thoroughly crooked job—"

"Somebody who knew the job," Mirella sang, "from serving a lot of time."

"Just about," I said. "And, damn it, he raises more questions than he answers."

EIGHTEEN

Because (as Mirella pointed out just before I could) it was impossible to imagine Horace FoFeality inventing a new and showily effective method of cloning humans.

"So he hired somebody," she said.

"Stop steaming," I said. "You're still irritated. Try it the other way around: somebody hired him. Your way, it's impossible: you can't hire somebody to make a new discovery."

"All right," she said. "So you're right and I'm steaming. That—Jerry, I got no words for what he is. I would say insect, I would say louse, but why insult a lot of small things maybe doing their best? That he was in here—in our house—telling our Totum what to do—poisoning our food—poisoning *your cooking—*"

"Relax," I said.

"It makes me want to disinfect everything," she said. "Maybe I will get over it. Give me a week. Anyhow a month."

"So somebody hired him," I said. "The interesting question isn't Who—"

"No?" Mirella said. "Me, Who is what I want to know."

"Who is always the question," I said. "File it, and go on. This time things are just a little different." I shut off the machine; we'd watched the rest of the trip, which was without incident.; the Totum had been gimmicked while turned off, and turned on again back at Boomerang Street. "What did somebody hire him *with?*"

"What else? Mirella said. "Money."

"Money isn't enough," I said. "He's a crooked bastard, and he's probably a greedy bastard—but he has a lot of money now. And he has a nice, showy title. He's right where he wants to be—and he's always been a cautious fellow, too. He wants to stay where he is."

"So in order to risk anything—"

"And it would have to be a risk," I said. "Even if all he did was abduct our Totum, there are no guarantees—I mean, we found him, and fast. So he would have to be grabbing for something big." I shrugged. "Money and power he's got. What else is there?"

She gave me a big grin. "There is always true love."

"Right," I said. "He's just the type."

"A type, there isn't," Mirella said. "But in order to have true love, I think you have to be a person. Human, Tock, Berigot, *somebody*. This FoFeality, who can believe he is a person? A yeast. A slime mold. Show me a slime mold has true love, I'll think twice about FoFeality."

"There's got to be something else," I said. "And maybe finding out what will tell us Who."

And of course there was, though true love came into it too— and in fact it did tell us Who. But locating it took a while.

Meanwhile, I put the back of my head to work on it, and Mirella, I'm sure, did whatever it is she does for the same purposes, and we went on with our lives. Very carefully.

Our lives, of course, were still focused closely on Amy-Robsart. The original Amy-Robsart. About her—whoever she was now—there were three questions to start with:

1. What, exactly, had been done to her?
2. Who had done it?
3. Why?

None of these questions looked like being anywhere near as formidable as tracking down Whoever (and of course the answers might *give* us Whoever). 1 had a good general answer: Somebody had developed a duplicating method that allowed not only of variations—according to Guy Finch all cloning or duplicating of anything complex enough did that—but of predictable variations. Amy-Robsart had been abducted, probably right from the damn garden, and duplicated with changes, and the rigged duplicate had been sent on back.

I had a number of possible answers to 3, of which the best seemed to be Amy-Robsart's influence over her father. He did listen to her; he indulged her; and she might tip the scales on any number of decisions he was making. The next question there was, of course: tip what particular scales, and for what particular purpose? But that opened up too many possibilities to be useful: the Emperor of the Comity makes decisions that affect other people the way most of us emit perspiration: sometimes a little, sometimes a lot, but damn seldom none at all.

2 was, of course, the real toughie. But a related question promised an approach to answering it:

What had happened to the original Amy-Robsart?

Maybe, of course, she'd been disposed of as soon as the duplicate had been declared ready to go. But that didn't seem altogether likely.

For one thing, I thought I had a vague handle on a way to do such duplicating—admittedly very vague, and while Guy Finch's lecture had been some help, it wasn't nearly help enough. But if my vague notion turned out to be the method being used . . .

Well, assuming the person who'd developed the method, and duplicated Amy-Robsart Berringer, was reasonably intelligent, he'd want insurance, of two different kinds. (And for "person" substitute "people", of course, as you like—or, of course, "slime molds".) First, he couldn't be finally, absolutely sure that the duplicate not only functioned, but was going to go right on functioning, and functioning the way he wanted it—her—to function. There were, as I'd been saying, no guarantees.

Suppose—the whole technique was something new, after all—there was an unexpected glitch somewhere in the process, and the duplicate simply collapsed into a puddle of goo after three days—or developed new and unwanted opinions or habits—or turned into Snow What, or Sinner Ella. Or, in fact, anything.

Maybe a second duplicate could then be made. But a new *substitution* might not be possible; that would depend on where the inventor was positioned, what the glitch was, when and where it became visible—and so on. If the inventor just happened to be very, very lucky he might manage a second substitution—but he'd have to have the original there to make his second-try duplicate from—the original, or enough data, of course. And complete data on a human being nineteen years old, with full memory, looked to be too bulky to be believable.

But if he were just slightly less lucky—if the glitch turned out showy enough, and long-lasting enough, to expose to anyone and everyone the fact that Amy-Robsart *wasn't* Amy-Robsart—

Then, he was much better off with a living Amy-Robsart than he could possibly be with a corpse. The living person might give him some bargaining power; a dead one could only get him executed.

Of course, the argument for killing the original was that a nonexistent original couldn't identify the person who'd done the duplicating. But, given the odds, it seemed more sensible to keep Amy-Robsart around, if at all possible—either as a template for the next duplicate, or as a bargaining chip in case of catastrophe.And if that was the way things worked out, it began to occur to me that the existence of an original Princess offered an interesting line of attack.

Where the Hell would you *keep* an abducted Princess?

NINETEEN

In a tower, of course—where she would sit sadly till her hair grew long enough. Then she could let the hair out of the tower window, and a passing Prince could rappel, or rapunzel, his way up to the room and rescue her. How the odds of rescue were improved by there being two people in a locked tower room, instead of one, I'd never been entirely sure, but possibly they could both rapunzel their way right down the hair again—of course cutting it off the Princess first, and braiding it to the window-bars, or wherever. The Prince could bring the scissors.

It made a charming picture, for a couple of seconds. But it seemed to me that there were other, and maybe more helpful, answers.

Wherever Amy-Robsart was being kept, it had to be close enough to the Palace to allow our Whoever to keep up with the latest news. And he'd have to be doing that first-hand—no news report, and not even a report from a handy confederate, would be detailed enough in all the right ways. If the duplicate started showing oddities—well, *what* oddities? Any change from pattern, however small, might be a red flag—immediate action might well be called for.

And he'd be right there to key two shots at me from a disassembled Robbie, too; that might have been a confederate—it might have been FoFeality, for that matter, though he didn't quite seem the type for any action that direct and open—but it didn't have to be. We weren't dealing with a mob, necessarily: everything so far could have been managed by a maximum of two people, and the numbers only got as high as two because FoFeality as Mad and Brilliant Inventor was a little too hard to swallow. Even the abduction—which was easier done by fraud than by force, perhaps helped out by a little drugging—didn't look like a job that needed an army, or even a small squad.

So Whoever had been right there, ready to jump in and do whatever seemed indicated—jog the duplicate a bit, make the duplicate disappear till a new one could be brought in, erase the duplicate and begin bargaining, with the original Amy-Robsart as his basic chip—any one of sixty actions.

Some of these possible actions were massively ugly, of course: murder, for instance, isn't any less murder because the person you've killed is a duplicate your lab constructed. (Or an innocent bystander your bolt happened to bite.) But I wasn't assuming that our clever little Whoever had any particular objections to any practical course of action; he might have, but he might just as easily be as amoral as an unprogrammed Robbie. So far, he'd put together a list that included kidnapping, murder, attempted poisoning, and abduction of a Totum; assuming he had scruples didn't look like the intelligent way to go.

All right, then: a nice, protected, soundproofed (of course) place within easy reach of the Palace—and without a lot of nosy neighbors. How many places like that could there be?

Unfortunately, the answer was: hundreds. I was sitting in one—my own apartment. The neighbors were a little closer than Whoever might have wanted them, but they weren't nosy types, and never had been—it was something I'd made sure of before moving in, years before. And my place was a long way from being unique.

Any further requirements? Any way to narrow the field?

None, not at the moment. Maybe something would occur to me.

As it happens, the big question hadn't really started to turn up in my head, not quite yet. I am not as bright sometimes as I am other times.

Right then, all I had was a Space to Let sign hanging in there. So I went looking for Mirella, and found her in the kitchen, arguing with our Totum.

The Totum was holding a Dockery glass in each hand, and I'll swear it looked stubborn.

"I told you," Mirella said. "Make the drinks, and put them in the pot."

The Totum stood there. A couple of seconds went by.

"Six times I told you," Mirella said.

I sighed. "The drinks program doesn't hook in to the cooking program," I said. "I told you that."

"I know it anyway," Mirella said. "I work with them too. But I figured, maybe there was a way to sidestep it."

"No way," I said. "Nothing covers putting drinks into a pot, or into the food. No call for it: null program."

She shrugged. "Worth a shot," she said.

"And it doesn't matter anyhow," I said. "It wasn't an eight-ounce glass of potassium cyanide, it was a small dose. Had to be."

She sighed, and nodded. "Well, I had to do something while I was thinking," she said. "Money and power. What else is there?"

"*Other* problems," I said. "Forget FoFeality's motive, whatever the Hell it was. For a while, anyhow. Look: where do you keep a kidnapped Princess while you duplicate her?"

"And afterward," she said. "Right. Has to be an afterward, if there can be: you want to play it very safe, kill only the ones who don't count at Court. The Knaves. Right." She sighed, shaking her round little head. "Maybe FoFeality has a big country place, he can keep her in a little dungeon."

"No—a place right here," I said. "Handy to the Palace." I laid it out, and Mirella nodded.

"So maybe he has one," she said. "FoFeality. A place right near the Palace."

"Maybe so," I said. "And maybe everybody involved does, damn it."

TWENTY

"We just might be able to get some answers, though," I said. "The trouble is—we have a list of suspects. FoFeality, the Finches, Claude Deke—"

"I will not believe Claude Deke," Mirella said.

"Neither will I, but let's leave him in. What's that old detective-story tag?"

"The least likeable person," Mirella said. "That is not Deke. That is FoFeality, no contest."

"Least likely," I said. "Anyhow, leave him in. Leave everybody in. Sunny Samuels. Greensinger. Godney Thrall. Who else?"

"The Emperor is out, the kids are out." She thought for a second. "Sten Rann is in."

"He's been with the Palace thirty-five years," I said.

"If Deke goes in, Rann goes in," Mirella said.

"Fine," I said. "Eight people. There might be a ninth—probably is, if Guy Finch isn't our inventor, and he doesn't look any better to me for the part than he does to you—but let's start with those eight. They've been visible, they've been around the situation."

"And do we know our Whoever isn't the inventor?" Mirella said.

"Unless he's Guy Finch, yes," I said. "He's had to be in contact with me somewhere along the line—just to know enough and get close enough. If the inventor's a stranger, there's no way he could also be the fellow who shot his bolts at me and poisoned our prawns."

"Person," Mirella said. "Not fellow."

"So we're looking for somebody we know, with a nice, convenient apartment close by."

"That," Mirella said, "is everybody. You think people like this, connected at the Palace, maybe even working in it, they have their houses six hundred miles away? Status thing: you hook in with the power, you live next door."

"Probably," I said, and as I did, the big question spotted my Space to Let sign, and began dickering about the mortgage.

"But we can find out," Mirella said. "There's a service, gives out any Somebody's address—so long as they give it to another Somebody."

"Right," I said. "Celebrity address people."

"And right now, you are a Somebody," she said. "For maybe five minutes. So call them, they'll tell you who is where, we can think it over from there."

So I did, and the people said they'd call back, and I tabled the question.

A slightly smaller question came along while the big one waited its damn turn.

Amy-Robsart Berringer had been duplicated, with changes—the changes being aimed at something the plotter or plotters wanted her to do, or say, or avoid.

The duplicating had resulted in an Amy-Robsart who was, visibly, not the same person. Hesitations, gaps, all the rest of it—all right, why? I'd been thinking about glitches turning up, and a small pile of them had—not enough for *everybody* to see that we had a Not-Quite-Amy-R. on our hands, but enough to make any halfway capable Whoever nervous.

Why hadn't the thing worked smoothly? Why, given the glitches, had it been tried at all?

Okay: it was something new, something somebody had just developed. A rough draft; there'd be bugs. Unexpected glitches, as I'd been thinking—well, you can't anticipate them all. But the big, showy ones, the ones that were visible instantly . . .

Well, my God, when you're busy working your little gimmick on the youngest (and quietest, to be sure) daughter of the Emperor of the Comity, don't you take care of the obvious bugs *first*? Duplicate some wandering human who won't be missed in a hurry—find out why your duplicating gimmick gives such odd results, and smooth out the process before you try it on somebody as visible as even the quietest daughter of the damn Emperor?

Of course you do. Which left, when I thought about it for a couple of seconds, just two reasons why there were bugs in the process, changes in Amy-Robsart Berringer that were noticeable (if not to those close to her, who *wanted* to believe Amy-Robsart was Amy-Robsart, at least to a few observant outsiders, like me and Mirella).

1. The bugs were built into the process: you couldn't do it at all without leaving traces. All you *could* do was set up the imperfect duplication, and then sit back, and hope nobody would notice.
2. You included the bugs deliberately—for what reason, I couldn't imagine at all.

It was obvious, by the time I'd reached that pair of odd answers, that I had far too many questions, and far too few facts.

The big question was still hiding away. It was not very closely related to one I'd already considered (and considered without getting anywhere at all): How had anybody been able to rig things to abduct my Totum, when nobody could have predicted just when and where the Totum was going to be out on the streets?

But those two were the important questions. I was spending my time on the smaller ones, but I didn't know that—and the small ones, as it turned out, were going to be my guidelines.

What I needed (I could see this much) was more facts. Well, I knew somebody who might have some.

We got Sten Rann out of a nice warm bed, and he was anything but eager to trot on over and chat. But a phone talk wasn't going to do it, and I wanted to leave the line clear in any case—the address people could leave a message on the Wait line, but you can't ask questions of a recorded message.

"Knave," he said wearily, "there can't be anything that won't wait till morning. Come to the Palace, ask for me, I'll be at your service—"

"It's important," I said, "and it's urgent. I need—we all need, and I'll explain—all the facts I can get, as fast as I can get them."

He said: "But surely—"

"I wouldn't call you if there weren't a rush," I said. "You're the Household Subchancellor. By rights I ought to be calling the Chancellor—"

"She's in Djakarta with the family," he said. "And I'm in bed."

"This is part of your job," I said. What the Hell, maybe it

was. I was firm enough, anyhow, to persuade Sten Rann, who appeared at my door less than an hour later. He looked a bit frazzled, but he also looked troubled, which was good. Things were changing: I wanted him even more troubled.

We sat him down, and Mirella had the Totum brew a pot of tea ("When I leave you, I'm going right on back to sleep," Rann said, "and coffee won't help"), and he said: "All right, Knave. What in God's name is so urgent?"

"Amy-Robsart," I said. "She's not."

He blinked, took a sip of tea, and said: "Not what?"

"She's somebody else," I said, and he said, of course: "An impostor?" and I laid things out for him.

He finished his first cup, and said: "She's been through a harrowing experience. Of course she's changed. But that doesn't—"

I shook my head. "What harrowing experience?" I said. "If she went sailing off the Keys, she had a perfectly calm time. And if she didn't—if she got snatched and returned—why isn't she saying that?"

He frowned. "And why isn't Sunny Samuels saying that?" he said. "She'd be bound to know—"

"She says she wasn't with Amy-Robsart, this trip."

Rann set the cup down. "She said that?"

"To me," I said. "And to Mirella. Here. Flatly."

"All right," he said. "Then where in God's name was she? She wasn't here. When Amy-Robsart—left—Sunny left too. We just assumed she'd gone off sailing with the Princess."

"She usually went sailing with her?" Mirella put in.

"Well, no," Rann said. "Usually Amy-Robsart went with— well, with someone from Security. I think Sunny liked being on dry land, is what it was; and Amy-Robsart was always thought-ful. *Is* always thoughtful. I mean—"

"Right. Sunny's story is unraveling very nicely," I said. "She told me she went sailing a lot. She also said she didn't go on this trip."

Rann was still frowning. "Why would she say things like that?"

"Because," I said, "something happened. To Amy-Robsart. Something that—well, she *isn't* Amy-Robsart. It's the only ex-planation that fits. And Sunny Samuels knows about it."

"You mean she did something—"

"I said she knows," I said. "And she may not know much: 'something happened, and keep quiet about it' may be the extent of what she knows. But I doubt she knows much more than that: if she'd been in on the whole thing, she'd have a better story. This is all improvised gabble—my God, all it took was one question to you and it fell apart."

"I'll have her head," Rann said.

"You'll have nothing, right now," I said. "She knows one more thing, and it's the most important thing. She knows who told her to keep quiet."

That square face could look very nicely grim. "She'll tell me," he said.

"She'll tell all of us," I said, "if we can figure out how to persuade her. But what's needed is for *everything* to unravel. Somebody is trying to pass off a fake Amy-Robsart on the Palace. We need to find the somebody."

"And we need to find the real Amy-Robsart," he said, and the phone rang.

TWENTY-ONE

I was expecting the celebrity-address people, but the voice was a reedy, odd, non-professional one I had just a little trouble identifying for a few seconds. "Knave? Knave? Is that you—"

"It's me," I said. "Who are—" and I had it. "Guy Finch. It's me, Guy. Why are you—"

"You've got to help me," he said, and burst into tears. Noisily.

I barked it into the phone: "What's happened?"

The tone brought him out of it a little, but his voice was still pretty shaky. "I need help," he said. "I need somebody's help. Maybe it's you. I hope it's you, Knave. Your number was in her notebook."

I spoke more gently. "Guy, you'll have to tell me what it is we're talking about. I might be able to help, but I need some facts."

"It's Mother," he said. "Somebody's—something's—" He took a deep breath. "Killed her," he said.

My first feeling was relief. Guy Finch in a panic over somebody might have been Guy Finch in a panic over Amy-Robsart Berringer. If somebody had to be dead (and apparently somebody was), I preferred it to have been Astarte Finch; I didn't have anything serious against the woman, but no matter what her influence as a hostess, her death wouldn't cause the massive whirlwind Amy-Robsart's would. (And the big question sat at the back of my head, laughing at me.)

Still . . .

"Somebody or something," I said. "Meaning what, Guy? Where are you?" One question at a time, to anybody in a panic—yes, but I thought he might just be able to handle those two at once.

He almost did. "Something," he said. "Something. It's—horrible. I'm where she is, Knave. Not in the same room. I couldn't stand to be in the same room. You can see that."

I took a deep breath myself. "Of course not," I said gently. "I'll come over right away. What's the address?"

"That's right, you've never been here," he said. His tone was a little less ragged, but it had gotten a little more distant;

Guy Finch was not in good shape. "We're—she's—it's 125 Robinson Brink. That's off the Oval—it's a big place, you can't miss—Knave, will you really come right over?"

"I'm leaving now," I said. "Don't do a thing. Don't even call anybody."

"Who would I call?" he said blankly.

"Nobody whatever," I said firmly, and hung up.

Sten Rann was staring at me. I realized I'd put the phone on Speaker automatically when I'd picked it up, figuring Mirella would have a Robbie ready to file the addresses the celebrity people were going to give me.

"My God," he said. "The police—"

"I'll take care of the police," I said, just as firmly. "This has got to be handled with care—or FoFeality will be all over it. He may be anyhow, but we'll do what we can." I turned to Mirella, who was punching instructions into a Robbie. "You're gong to have to stay here, damn it," I said.

She nodded. "Figures," she said. "First, this kid will not take kindly to two people, especially if one of them is female. With female people he is not real comfortable. That, anybody can see."

"We'll put it together later," I said, and she nodded.

"Second," she said, "I can wait for the addresses, right? The Robbie is taped for them, I'll dig anything else out I can, and when you get back we'll figure."

"Right," I said. I looked back at Sten Rann. "All right," I said. "I'll report to you as soon as I can; you're going to have to know about this."

He was still staring at me. "Knave," he said, "what am I supposed to do now? Astarte Finch—"

"Go home and get some sleep," I said. "But not much." He looked at me as if I'd gone crazy, or as if he had.

125 Robinson Brink was a small mansion, if there is such a thing, overlaid roof to ground in some synthetic that gave the whole place an aggressive pink glow. On most worlds, houses are built of stone or brick or cement or wood (or local equivalent), sometimes of metal—or, of course, thrown together out of combinations of such stuff—and that's about it, except for a paint job and, maybe, a field of some kind. But Earth, which

tends to think of itself as a fashion leader, has gone in for some damn odd stuff, the last century or so.

The underpinnings of this place were probably stone and metal, or cement and metal; but everything was covered by whatever it was that glowed pink into the night. The windows had been left as clear glassex, and most of them were lit. The place was two stories high, and one full block wide—maybe half a block deep—and the front was grandly disturbed by pillars, openwork gates, animal heads sculpted and then dressed in the pink sheeting, and a lawn that seemed, in the combined light of the Moon, a couple of streetlamps and the house, a vague and sinister purple.

The large front gate was ajar, and I went past it, and between two pillars, to the front door. That was shut tight—a solid-looking thing eight or nine feet high, covered with abstract carvings, and just as pink as everything else. I looked for the bell-announce, and found it high up on the left, disguised as a bunch of stonework leaves. I pushed the thing; if it made a sound inside the place, I couldn't hear it.

A car whizzed by, on its way to anywhere. The sound made the house, set on its great damn lawn, seem even more lonely. There were dark bulks off in the distance to either side—other houses, where everybody was either asleep or gone somewhere else for the year.

Time passed. I pushed the bell-announce again. After a while, I gave the door a whack, and the thing opened within seconds, and very fast. Either it wasn't as heavy as it looked, or it had the Hell of a mechanical system to back it up.

Guy Finch was standing in the doorway, breathing hard and looking lost. He was wearing a light-blue jumper that had seen better years, and his blond hair was a large and showy birds'-nest. His hornrimmed glasses were more or less in place, and behind the lenses his odd yellow eyes each looked about a foot wide. They blinked at me, and his mouth opened and closed like a guppy's.

"It's me, Guy," I said gently. "I'm here."

"Oh," he said. "Knave. Right. Knave. I'm sorry; nobody was here, I had to come down and open the door, and it took time. We have to do something. You can see that—we have to do something."

"Right," I said. I went past him into the entrance hall. "Let's start with what happened, shall we?"

"What happened," he said blankly. He looked down at his hand, and seemed surprised to find a door attached to it. He pushed, and the door swung shut. I expected a dull boom, but heard nothing but the hiss of air as the machinery worked. "I called you. Because we have to do something. Someone has to help."

I had to phrase it carefully; Guy was an inch away from hysteria, and I wasn't at all sure whether he was an inch before it or an inch into it. "When you called me," I said, "you told me you weren't in the same room with her. Were you in the next room?"

He considered it. "I think so," he said at last. I nodded.

"Then let's go there," I said, "and we can discuss what has to be done."

He led the way, thank God—I hadn't been sure he'd take direction at all—across the showily bare entrance hall to an immense, curving staircase. Inside, the glowing pink had been replaced by glowing ivory walls, but the staircase was alternate risers of green and gold. We went up—the thing looked like the sort of staircase heroines made grand entrances from, in 3V costume stuff—turned left in a hall a little dimmer than the downstairs, and stopped at the second door. "I called from here," he said. "It's a study, there's a phone in it."

"Very convenient," I said, and opened the door. We went in, and I was three steps into the room before I took it in, and stopped dead.

TWENTY-TWO

The walls were lined with bookshelves, and the shelves were filled with books, most of them in sober, uninviting-looking bindings and looking as untouched as if they'd lived out their little lives behind transparent walls. The room was furnished with overstuffed couches, a few chairs, two ornamental-looking desks and a lot of small tables, and lighting was an overhead array, with small lamps on a few of the tables. None of this made much of an impression on me, then or ever.

What made an impression was the Totum standing quietly in the far right corner. It was either switched to inactive or had burned out, because not even the attention lights were lit. But the room lighting was good enough to show me the splashes of blood on the casing.

Guy either didn't see them, or was blanking out on the Totum completely. He walked almost casually to one of the tables, where a phone set rested, and sat down in the chair next to it. "Here's where I called from," he said, "Now, we'll have to do something."

"Right," I said. I drifted over toward the Totum. I wasn't sure Guy even knew the thing was in the room; he barely knew I was. He'd be coming out of his shock soon, I thought, and he didn't figure to be coming out well. The job was to neutralize him before that happened. "You told me she'd been killed," I said carefully. "How did you know?"

"Know?" he said. "Everything. All the blood. Everything. What else could she be? Knave—"

"I want you to go downstairs," I said slowly and clearly, "and lock the front door. In a little while the bell will ring, and it will be some officials. I want you to wait right there and let them in."

"Officials?" he said. "Bell?"

"The doorbell," I said. "The bell-announce. They'll be officials here to take charge of things. To straighten everything out." I thought of how to phrase it. "To make sense," I said.

He stared at me. "Really?"

I nodded. "Are you wearing a watch?"

He looked to see, and nodded.

"Good," I said. "I want you to keep your eye on the watch. I need to know exactly when you get to the front door, when you lock it, and when—to the second—the bell rings and you open the door for the officials."

"Exactly," he said. "To the second."

"Right," I said. Give a scientist a thoroughly technical job to do (whether or not it makes any sense), and he may stay calm. If the job locates him in one spot, and focuses his attention on one thing—like a watch—you may have a chance of keeping him calm when shock wears off. God knows it wasn't a certainty, but a chance was the best bet I had. "What time is it now?"

He looked at the watch again. "It's—" He stopped, blinked and looked again. "Eleven-sixteen. And thirty-one seconds. Thirty-two."

"Good," I said. "Leave now. Don't call the time out to me, but remember it—exactly when you get to the door, exactly when you lock it, exactly when the bell rings—"

"Exactly when I let them in," he said. "Now?"

"Now," I said. "There's no time to lose." And he was gone—moving, I was glad to see, with fair speed, and a little more confidently than he had been. I left the door open, took one deep breath, and picked up the phone.

Sten Rann, of course. I'd told him he wouldn't get much sleep, but that turned out to be too hopeful a notion: he hadn't even had a chance to get home, but his pocket piece was on, and once he'd heard my fast description of the scene he agreed to everything I suggested without argument.

He arrived twenty-five minutes or so later, with three outriders. Two of them were filler—one male, one female, detailed to stick with Guy Finch, question him, talk to him, hold his hand or do anything indicated, for a while, to keep him reasonably calm and absolutely located. I'd specified two dependable types, and felt I could trust Rann to supply fairly helpful people; a Subchancellor for something like the Palace has to have a lot of varied people more or less instantly on tap.

The third was a gamble—I hadn't known whether Rann could find such a person, or, indeed, whether one even existed. That the Columbus police would include people skilled with

Totums and Robbies went without saying; that there was one such skilled person who had no ties whatever to Horace FoFeality, and who could be trusted to keep his mouth shut, was no more than a hope. If FoFeality had built up one class of close acquaintances—not counting his political clients and hangers-on—that class consisted of police, of all sorts; and the degree of acquaintanceship (I couldn't really think of him as having friends) had to be greater since he'd become Palace Security chief.

But Rann had managed to fill the order—almost—and the lack was the result of my own carelessness. The police expert who came with him, and with me, up the damn grand staircase to the library next to the murder room, wasn't guaranteed to keep his mouth shut. The expert—Meerande Fellm—was (Rann assured me) guaranteed to keep *her* mouth shut.

She wasn't only female—very—but, as the name may have told you, a Mlang. I hadn't known there were non-human people on the Columbus police force, but Meerande (we got to first names instantly, but it didn't mean friendly relations, exactly—or unfriendly ones either) told me there were even two Berigot working in History Access—doing essentially library work, which is what Berigot are better at than humans will ever be. There was a Giell, too, just hired in from Ravenal and working as consultant to the Psychological section.

Mlangs were somewhat more common—though how much more it would be hard for the casual observer to say. I may have met a few Mlangs here and there (they're great travelers, and can be found almost anywhere), but I'm not sure—and, to be brutally frank, neither are you, unless you're the sort of unfriendly person who asks new acquaintances for IDs. They don't hide the fact that they're non-humans—in fact, if anything, they seem rather proud of it, viewing homo sapiens as Somebody's unsuccessful try at duplicating Mlangs (it's said that—wildly unlikely as this sounds—Mlangs and humans can actually crossbreed), but they don't advertise it, either. They seem to feel that, if the fact comes up in conversation, fine, and if it doesn't, there are six or seven thousand more interesting things to talk about.

You may, as I say, have met a Mlang or two. On the other hand, you may only have met the same number of striking-looking human beings. Humans are very varied, for height, weight, color, shape of nose and a staggering list of other details; Mlangs run much more to a single set of types, though coloration varies, as do height and weight—as if, somewhere along the line, a mad geneticist had regularized the race once and for all.

This isn't, as far as anyone knows (as far as Mlangs know, too, or will admit even to careful researchers with lots of access to Mlang records), anything like the case. But they do run very firmly to a very few types, and Meerande was a fine sample of one type.

She was just my height—six feet even—and weighed about what I do, give or take eight pounds. Her figure would have been startlingly showy, though far from impossible, in a human; her face, quiet, severe and basically calm—despite large, brilliant green eyes—looked somewhat confused and withdrawn; and her hair was the usual Mlang display—a big cascade of (in her case) brilliant, eye-stopping red.

Rann introduced us, gave me a fast sketch of Meerande's background and trustworthiness, and said: "The body. For God's sake, Knave, the body."

"I haven't even seen it yet," I said, "and I don't think it's likely to be a pleasant sight, even as dead bodies go. Guy Finch said 'something' killed her—and he may have been right, more or less—and he talked to me about 'all the blood and everything'. We can go and look later—though let's not disturb anything until we figure out what the Hell to do—but the first thing to look at isn't the body."

"No," Meerande said. Her voice was the slightly droning contralto typical of female Mlangs—again, unusual but not impossible in humans. "I understand why my presence has been requested." She walked toward the blood-spattered Totum.

"Hold it," I said. "Sooner or later this whole damn mansion is going to be a crime scene, and we don't want more disturbance of it than we can help."

"In other words," Meerande said, "what can we know from visual and olfactory inspection of the Totum, and that only. Quite so, Knave."

I blinked. "Olfactory?" I said.

"Smell lingers," she said. "Odors are important indicators

of many things. Mr. Rann's nervousness, your own sense of confusion and haste—these are quite apparent, to even an average Mlang nose. And mine is quite well trained, Knave. Quite well trained."

A small cascade of images having to do with trained noses—jumping through hoops, sneezing on command—shot through my head and was banished with dispatch. I nodded as soberly as I could manage, and said: "I see."

"But the first fact of importance is simply visual," Meerande said—and as she did her voice changed just a trifle. Having read up a little on Mlangs here and there over the years, I knew what had happened: Rann and I had effectively disappeared from her universe, which now contained only Meerande and the Totum. Speech to me, or to Rann, would be little more than reporting back over immense distances to anonymous observers.

They're what a psychiatrist friend of mine describes as "problem-oriented": given a problem to think about or work on, they focus on it so entirely that attention to anything else in the surround simply vanishes, sometimes for hours or even days at a time.

Again, unusual but not impossible, among humans—and standard, among Mlangs.

"All right," I said "What is it?"

"The Totum has been turned off," she said.

TWENTY-THREE

This seemed to me too obvious to discuss. "That," I said, "we can all see."

Meerande's voice remained abstracted. She was standing about four feet from the Totum, staring at it fixedly. "No," she said. "What is obvious to any observer is that it is not operating: all indicators are negative, and its attention lights are off."

"Oh," I said, but she was going on:

"What is obvious to a trained observer is that the machine is not malfunctioning; it has been turned off. The state of the vision and handling elements makes that clear."

I nodded. "How?" I said. I was willing to take her word for the fact, if I had to; but I feel a lot more cheerful, any time and any place, if I can follow even an expert's reasoning.

"Note the completely shuttered vision elements," she said, "shuttered, but lacking a double seal. Note the position of the handling manipulators: curled slightly inward, not rigidly splayed."

Anyone but an expert would have said eyes and fingers, of course. Is your Totum a living thing? Not if you're an expert in the area; then it's a mechanical device. I've noticed the same habit—just slightly less intrusive—among those experts on human mechanisms, doctors. It isn't universal, but it is depressingly common.

I nodded again. I should have noticed that much myself—I'm not an expert, but I'm not completely ignorant; I own the things, and in a simple barefoot way I can sometimes even repair them.

"But the process has not quite been completed," she said. "In a complete shutdown, there are no such signs: one may turn off a Totum temporarily, but shutting it down assumes a larger time before re-use; and if the Totum simply ceases operation for some other reason, that larger time must be assumed, for safety. The handling manipulators splay; the vision elements are double-sealed." She shook her head, very slightly. "No, what we have here is a Totum that has been turned off temporarily—either with the design of turning it on again after a brief while, or out of carelessness or haste. If a complete shutdown were wanted, the recognition signal would also have been turned off—this requires some technical facility but is not quite beyond capability for the average user."

"Haste sounds good," Rann said. "My God, the thing had just committed a murder. I'd have turned it off in the Hell of a hurry, myself—my God, I'd have bashed its head in."

"It did not commit murder—nor involve itself in whatever bloody deed has left its residue on the casing—without direction," Meerande said. "Someone instructed it to do whatever it did. The mechanism—like a gun or a knife—is guiltless."

Rann said it again: "My God." Then he added: "They're supposed to be harmless."

Meerande made a sound like a small, well-bred snort. "There exist no harmless objects," she said, "and no harmless mechanisms. A piano is not a lethal instrument—but people have been killed by pianos, in at least two ways."

"Right," I said. "The thing falls on you—or the piano wire gets used to strangle you."

"Exactly," Meerande said. "Nothing is harmless: a sheet of ordinary fax paper may cut; a bite of food may choke. We live, all of us, in a dangerous world; that a complex mechanism like a Totum can provide danger, and harm, should not be surprising."

"Basic safeties exist," Rann said. "A Totum can't hurt a human being. If a Totum sees a human being who needs help—"

"The Totum will call for help," I said, "over the recognition circuit. Alerting every other mechanical in range, and any human who can be informed by a mechanical."

"All quite true," Meerande said.

"If you took off a Totum's arm and beat someone to death with it," Rann said, "you'd have to turn the Totum on to reattach the arm—right?" Meerande nodded. "And as soon as it was turned on, it would notice the person you'd been clubbing—and send out its alarm."

"Quite true," Meerande said. "The Totum would be guiltless, and helpful. But not harmless; there exist no harmless objects in this universe." Her lecturing tone, though a simple contralto drone rather than a weary rasp, reminded me suddenly of an old—well, friend may not quite be the word. Meerande sounded a lot like Master Higsbee—which (because I think of the Master as the man who knows everything that can possibly be known) was partly reassuring, and which (because the Master is the most irritating person I have ever met) was also partly bothersome.

All the same, she was (like the Master, damn it) saying something true and useful. Rann nodded slowly. "Maybe so," he said. "Somebody pointed the thing, aimed it and fired it."

"We do not know that the Totum acted, in any way," Meerande said. "We know that something resembling human blood, on visual and olfactory inspection, is splashed on its casing; we know that one greatly disturbed human has said that 'something' killed another human, nearby."

"And the rest is speculation," I said, "until we find out a little more."

"Not quite all the rest," Meerande said. "The Totum has been in close contact with a male human, in a state of great anxiety—anxiety perhaps well controlled, perhaps not. This contact has been fairly recent—within the last two hours."

"Smell?" I said. She nodded slightly.

"Smell," she said. "It is indistinct—not wholly fresh, and overlain by other odors—but it is human and male."

"Guy Finch," Rann said tiredly. "No surprise: anxiety is one word for the state he's in. Not a strong enough word, but a start."

"Not Guy," I said. "I talked with him. He didn't know the Totum was in the room. He never went near it—and if he had, he wouldn't have said something killed Astarte Finch. He'd have said the Totum did it."

"Maybe so," Rann said again. "But another man—the killer? The person who directed or programmed the Totum to kill?"

"Or did the killing himself, while the Totum stood by," Meerande said. "I should like to approach the body."

"Anything more you can tell about the Totum?" I said.

"Not from visual and olfactory evidence alone," she said. "But from a similar examination of the body, I should be able to add to our knowledge of the activities of the Totum."

Rann said: "Pleasant or not, we're going to have to."

"And we're going to have to figure out how to do an end-run around FoFeality, too," I said. Then I nodded. "All right. Body first, plotting later."

TWENTY-FOUR

Astarte Finch lay on the bed, holding a bottle. It's a peaceful sort of description, but the bed and the bottle were the only peaceful things about it. Astarte, even in death, looked like a war zone.

She had been very thoroughly bashed, mostly about the body: there was enough left of the head and face to allow of eyeball identification, and there was no doubt the thing on the bed *was* Astarte. She seemed to have some broken ribs, at least one broken leg and a badly shattered right arm—but her right hand held on to the bottle.

There was blood everywhere, and there was blood on the bottle, too. It was a fancily expensive, glass wine bottle—full, and tightly corked. The label was smeared with drying blood, and impossible to read.

The bed was a tumbled mess of sheets and quilts, all streaked and spattered with blood; it was one of those canopied jobs, and the bedposts were dark wood, very fancily carved. Astarte was wearing what looked like a robe over a lacy nightgown, and one felt slipper—the other one, I saw after a while, was off in a corner of the room.

The room wasn't as large as, say, a ballroom, but for a bedroom it was extensive, and not too crowded. Bed, dressing-table, wardrobes, chairs (two with ottomans), a small sofa, three different floor-length mirrors. The windows were shut, sealed—and curtained in a royal-purple fabric that looked as shiny as satin and as heavy as lead. Lighting was from the ceiling, with lamps (unlit) on the dressing-table and on a small table by the sofa.

I wandered around, carefully, touching nothing. Meerande did the same, her face forward, doing her own visual (and olfactory) search.

Rann stood by the door, moaning just a little and saying: "Oh my," under his breath at intervals. He wasn't quite wringing his hands, and he wasn't quite throwing up, but staying on the right side of both took great control; he was sweating as if he'd been standing in a sauna.

"The Totum has been in this room," Meerande said after a

little while, "and so has a man. Indications are confused; the smell of blood is overpowering—but a man was certainly here, within the last hour or a little more."

"The same man?" Rann said in a choked voice.

Her head shook, just a little. "I cannot tell," she said. "The indications on the Totum were indistinct; and here there are too many odors both strong and conflicting."

"Might have been Guy in here, then," I said. "He must have come to the doorway at least, to see the body."

"Yes, he was at the doorway," she said; "his fear and confusion remain there. He leaned against the right-hand lintel. But he did not approach nearer; so much fear and confusion would leave traces perceptible even through the cyclone of smells here."

"And the other man came closer?" I said. She nodded. "You said the body would tell you more about the Totum," I went on.

"It tells me the Totum itself may actually have touched the body—beyond such slight contact as would leave little trace," she said. "Traces of its presence exist on it, and not on the bedclothes."

I blinked. "The woman's been knocked around pretty heavily," I said. "A Totum would have the strength—"

"So would a human," she said. "Proximity is not causation. A human armed with a club of some sort, perhaps—or with strong enough arms and hands to use those alone. Though there is an odd odor, I believe—masked by the strength of other odors, but present."

"An odd odor?" I said, thinking of poisons.

"Fax paper," she said. "It is identifiably fax paper. Very hard to distinguish, but present. At least five standard sheets, possibly as many as thirty, unwrapped and open to the air.'"

I thought of Astarte Finch being beaten to death with a club made of nice, thick, shiny fax paper. I put that set of pictures away, but I filed the oddity, of course. You could kill somebody with fax paper—drop a few reams on him from a height—but a) it would take a fantastic barrage of bound reams of the stuff to do the damage visible on Astarte Finch, and b) if there *had* been such a barrage, where the Hell was the fax paper now? You'd have needed a forklift and a truck to cart away the pile that would have been needed, and disposing of it in the room without leaving, say, a very, very large heap of ashes seemed to call for something showy in the line of magic.

And Meerade had said between five and thirty sheets, no more.

"Did she fight him off?" I said. "The man who was here, I mean."

Meerande shrugged. "I cannot tell," she said. "If he bled, for instance, visual and olfactory examination cannot distinguish his blood from hers; laboratory analysis may be helpful, later on. If the man was wounded, he did not feel great fear regarding it."

"Anxiety?" I sad.

"There was great anxiety present in the other room," she said. "It seems to be present here to a lesser degree. But any person committing such an act would display anxiety, at the least."

"Rage, maybe," Rann said.

"Rage is not present," she said, which interested me a great deal.

There wasn't much more to get, and we went back into the other room for discussion. First on the agenda, of course, was FoFeality.

Legal standing in the case was of course held by the Columbus police, not by Palace Security. But, given the kind of influence Astarte Finch had tossed around, and (after some years of hostessing) her undoubted connections in the Palace and around it, the Columbus police were going to be firmly, and instantly, under the thumb of FoFeality's Security people—unless we could shove Horace FoF. out of the damn way.

"We might," Rann said cautiously, "send him off somewhere to investigate something. Or to talk to the Emperor at Djakarta. That'd keep him out of things pretty well."

"It would," I said, "except he wouldn't go. In the Emperor's absence, I am damned if I know who'd have the authority to send him anywhere—"

"The Minister for Justice, I think, in a criminal case," Meerande said.

"And we haven't got time to persuade the Minister—whoever that is just now, I haven't kept up with local politics—and no way of knowing whether he *can* be persuaded," I said. "This has to be something we can do on our own, that takes FoFeality out of the play, and keeps him out."

"Well," Rann said very slowly, "we could make some clues. Leading to—someplace far away. Get him to notice those clues, and start him looking in a different—"

"Tamper with evidence at a crime scene?" Meerande said. "The waters would be muddied—any chance of apprehending the real criminal here might well be lost."

I may just have tampered with evidence myself, a time or two—in one good cause or another—but I agreed with her; it's not the sort of thing you want to do casually, or (if possible) at all.

The Totum stood in its corner, a dead hulk, and watched us—or that's what it felt like to me. Not, undoubtedly, to Meerande. We tossed a few more bad ideas around, and then I had a good one.

I looked at the other two solemnly, and quoted one sentence from my scrappy Classical education:

"I'll make him an offer he can't refuse."

TWENTY-FIVE

The rest of the job was comparatively simple: keeping matters completely quiet until I had a chance to neutralize FoFeality. Guy was easy: Rann's people could stay with him as long as needed, Rann told me. "They'll stay quite a while anyhow," he said. "My God, Knave, the kid's in no sort of shape to be alone."

"Right," I said, and dismissed Guy from my mind—for a while. There were questions, but this wasn't the time to start asking them. Rann's people would of course share him with the police, when Guy got to a state where answers might, now and then, follow any questions at all. "But Meerande here will have some explaining to do to her people."

She shrugged. It's rather an abrupt, mechanical gesture among Mlangs. "I have touched nothing, I have disturbed nothing," she said in that contralto drone. "There is nothing to show that I was here—except the testimony of you two, Mr. Rann's two other attendants, and Guy Finch. Finch can be ignored; he can perceive little, in his present state, and remember less. The two attendants—"

"Will keep their mouths damned well shut," Rann said flatly, and I believed him.

Meerande shrugged again. "Then there is no problem," she said. "I was never here."

"And you weren't, either," I told Rann. "I was, but I'll cover that, when and if I have to—no trouble. Guy called me; the rest is talk. The thing to do is to get FoFeality out of the way fast, so the scene doesn't have a chance to cool off any more than it has."

That appeared to require finding him, late at night, and shoving him away from things—which sounded harder to do than, in fact, it turned out to be.

But, of course, when I got back home, there was Mirella with her list. The celebrity-services people had phoned back, and she had all the addresses. Of course one of them was Our Horace's, and—taking time out for about six bites of a sandwich, and a cup and a half of good coffee—Mirella almost has the touch for it, after some lessons from me—and a snippet or two of casual conversation with my other lobe, to bring her up to

speed, I headed out to 1 Grandview Terrace. It was then just after midnight.

It isn't quite as fancy a place as the 1 and the Grand would seem
to hint at, but—well, it ain't just, as the ancients used to say,
minced livers. 1 Grandview Terrace (now owned and operated,
as they say, by a nice family I've never met) was a pile of stone
and glassex in what architectural historians refer to, God
knows why, as Cheesy Modrun. The basic walls were stone,
there were a lot of glassex panels sticking out either as outside
passageways (breezy-ways, the Ancients called them, apparently because they look like a sort of light-hearted after-
thought) or just as showy panels leading nowhere; the corners
and rooftop edges were bordered in little white lights—hundreds of the damn things, not enough to give a glare or even a
decent glow but showy as all getout—and the ground-floor windows, so help me, were edged in gold leaf. Lacquered over or
some such damn thing, I suppose, but very shinily gold.
    It was, all in all, almost as ugly as Horace himself, and an
entirely fitting container for him. I hope to God the new owners
have toned it down some; it lives in a nice neighborhood that
doesn't really need an eyesore.
    I hadn't called ahead; I hadn't done anything whatever
ahead; I just marched up past a glassex panel on my left hand,
got to the massive oak front door, and pushed the bell-announce. It was a gold button, rather large, with a gold blazon
over it that said *FoF.* My sentiments exactly.
    Time passed. I leaned on the bell some more. Maybe he was
out on the town somewhere, practicing his semicomputer billiards or, of course, doing something more repulsive. But I had
to give him every chance.
    Finally a speaker over the door cleared its throat and a con-
tralto voice said: "Who is there?"
    Not Horace's voice, of course. "Gerald Knave," I told the
speaker. "To discuss robotics with Mr. Feality."
    Long pause. "Mr. FoFeality," the speaker said, giving the
Fo just the slightest emphasis, "is not presently—" and a new
voice cut in.
    "Knave?" Horace FoFeality said in a slightly weary voice,
even hoarser than usual. "It's—Good Lord, man do you know

what time it—"

"I know it's late," I said. "It's almost *too* late. We'd better talk. About robots. Totums in particular."

Short pause. "Poona will let you in," he said, and I waited. Thirty or forty seconds later the door clicked and opened, and a small dark woman bowed at me.

I gave her a friendly smile. "Poona?"

"That is I, Sir," she said, in a lovely, liquid contralto. "Please to follow along now."

She shut the door behind me, and set out down a dimly lit hallway. After a while we came to a small door—painted gold, of course—and she opened it.

"Please to step into the inside of," she said, and opened the door to a small cubicle.

What the Hell, maybe poison gas would come out of the ceiling. Maybe this was how Horace disposed of his enemies, when and as possible. But that seemed just a trifle improbable, so I walked through the doorway. Poona shut the door, there was a little whir, and the room rose.

Simple, old-fashioned elevator, of course. It was rather a slow one, as most private elevators seem to be, but it only had one flight to rise, and when it stopped I pushed at the door. It swung open, and I stepped out into what I suppose was Horace's sitting-room.

Or preening-room. It was set up very much the way the club I'd first met him at had been set up—leather couches, polished dark-wood tables, dim but sufficient overhead lighting, a chair here and there, and two walls full of printed books, spools, tapes and the like. There was one big window on a third wall, looking out onto a rear garden.

Horace was standing by the window. He turned when the elevator door opened, and gave me a big imitation of a smile. "Always glad to see you, Knave," he said. "Always glad, any hour, day or night, you know. How have things been among the Survivor fraternity? If, that is—if you have any tales you can tell to a poor groundling, of course."

"Things," I said, "have been just a trifle strained. I need a favor from you, Mr. Feality."

"FoFeality," he said equably, in his hoarse little mutter. "I prefer it—as you prefer Knave to, say, Mr. Knave. Let us be polite, let us by all means be polite, isn't that the best way after all?"

I shrugged. "Whatever the name, I really do need this favor."

Horace was in the driver's seat. I could see him thinking that, as he shuffled the smile offstage and replaced it with a grave, thoughtful expression just as false. "I'll be happy to do what I can," he said. "Anything at all, for one of our brave boys out on the front lines of the colonies, you know. Anything at all."

I didn't say it. It was a strain, but I didn't say: "What you can do is nothing, you do it very well, and please keep on doing it." I had to bite it back, and I bit bravely: damn it, there was a time and a place for the simple pleasures of life, and insulting Horace was going to have to wait.

Instead, I said: "There's been a murder."

If he already knew about it, he hid the fact nicely. "Murder?" he said flatly. "And you need the help of Palace Security?"

"Not exactly," I said. "I need your help. You, personally. Horace FoFeality."

"Well," he said. And waited, doing a fair job of not looking both triumphant and expectant. "Who has been killed? Let's start there, if we can. Always best, starting from the start—don't you find it so?"

"We can, and I do," I said. "Astarte Finch is dead. And what I need from you—"

"Astarte? Dear Astarte?" he said calmly. "Good Lord, Knave, that's terrible news. Just terrible." He took a breath. "She was a lovely woman, lovely. One of a kind, you might say. One of a kind."

I remembered the manic drunk I'd first met. "Indeed," I said. "There'll be an investigation, of course. She was close to many people in the Palace—"

"Almost all, I should say."

"—but the Columbus police are doing the investigating. They'll handle matters."

He pursed his lips. The man of power, considering all the facts. "I don't see why this should be left to what is, after all, only a local policing force, you know—nothing more than that—they have no Palace standing, as such, and in this case, given the fact that Ms. Finch was, as you say, close to many people in the—"

"That's the favor," I said. "Let them have the case. Let them handle it. Completely. Stay out of it."

His lips got pursier. "In a case of this importance—" he began.

"Or else," I said.

"Or else what?" The face was a stone mask, and the little eyes glittered.

"Or else I'll make some tapes public," I said. "Tapes that show you tampering with a Totum belonging to me. Tapes—"

He must have checked the case for taping equipment, but the surprise never showed. Horace had been around, after all. "Tampering? Knave, I'm afraid I simply don't understand."

I sighed. "Try this," I said. "I had the Totum rigged—never mind how—and it made a nice clean record of your theft of it. It blanked out when you started working on it, of course, and didn't return till you put it back on course—but every second of the theft itself is there." He looked disbelieving. "And your face comes through very nicely," I added. "The whole damn sequence does—right down to the repair work going on, and the pedestrian path the Totum took, there on Boomerang Street, where you grabbed it."

That did it, of course. He glared at me. "Knave," he said, "this is blackmail." He started to say sixty or seventy more words, and chopped them all off.

I gave him his own smile back. "You should know," I said.

TWENTY-SIX

After a second, he said: "Well. Let's consider this. Let us consider, Knave. By all means. Consider. Yes." A pause. "Why do you want—"

"Columbus police to handle this particular case?" I said. "Does it matter? I want it that way, and I think I'm going to have it that way."

And maybe I was, at that. We left it there—a few more sentences on either side, but nothing worth reporting—and I went away with my fingers and toes crossed.

Horace, after all, was more than capable of doing a little crossing—double-crossing—himself, at any time, if he thought he saw a way to make it work. The Totum's records would stop him for a small while—and if he doubted their existence I could dub him a copy with no trouble—but he might wiggle his way clear, somehow or other. Wiggling, damn it, was one of his major talents.

The easiest way to wiggle free and keep his thumb on the case, of course, would be to plant somebody on the investigative team—somebody who'd be quietly reporting to Horace, and who would, just as quietly, take Horace's orders if he wanted anything done about the case. Or about anything else.

Horace would have friends on that force, naturally; Horace had made a career of finding such handy friends. I knew I could trust Sten Rann, and I thought, both on his say-so and on my own first look at her, that I could trust Meerande Fellm. Anybody else might be Horace, wearing a mask.

And of course he'd have an extra motive for interference— not only keeping his fingers in the Palace pie, so to speak, but watching out for Number One—since Horace himself was certainly involved somehow with Amy-Robsart's little transformation.

Well, there was nothing to be done about it except file the possibility. I dug out my pocket piece, woke up Sten Rann with the news that the Columbus police could go ahead without immediate fear of bother from the Palace, and went home. It was late, I was tired, and I wanted only to find a bed to fall down on; but when I got home Mirella was just finishing with the Totum.

She'd had the thing in pieces all over the floor, apparently, but it was now being slapped together again. She put on the last fragment of case, turned to me and said: "Welcome home. I thought maybe a simple check."

I'd been busy, and it hadn't occurred to me, but of course she was right.

"Find anything?"

"An expert I am not," she said, "but recorders I could recognize. Maybe this FoFeality has come up with a gimmick—he's good with machines, right?—but it would have to be a very new gimmick and also a very small gimmick. If not, and I figure not, the Totum is clean."

Which did not mean that it hadn't been instructed to put an eye&ear someplace in the apartment, damn it—just before poisoning the prawns. Everything we said and did might be transmitted to Horace's files—or to somebody's files.

It was something to worry about in the morning, and I said so. "I'll fill you in then, too," I told Mirella. "It has been a long, long day."

"Like six years of it," she said. "So let's turn in. Whatever you got, and whatever we need to get, morning will do for it."

Morning, of course, was horrible. I am not a morning person, even at the best of times, and neither is Mirella. This simplified matters: we weren't in any kind of shape to defeat an eye&ear when we woke up, but we also weren't in any kind of shape to do or say anything meaningful. We exchanged grunts and nods—I sometimes think I evolve rapidly through the average day, climbing up from Neanderthal grunting and sign language in the mornings to whatever approximation of h. sapiens I manage to reach later on—and I went and prepared coffee, pretty much on automatic, while Mirella brewed tea.

We'd left the telltale on, of course, and when we got breakfast to the table and nothing flashed blue, we sat and ate in silence for a while.

Then we began to talk over the events of the day before, and my visit with Horace. We talked quite openly—we even discussed the details of the interference net I was going to set up, after I'd done the dishes, to scramble any possible eye&ear reception. I'd stocked a few language tapes on my ship—I usually have four or five—and Mirella had had plenty of time to study them en route to Earth. She studies things with blinding speed, when interested—and there isn't a lot she isn't interested in.

We talked things over in Saurian, which is (except on Rasmussen itself) spoken, I think, by three or four people in the universe. I'd had professional dealings with the Rasmussen saurians, years before, and visited occasionally; Mirella may be the only non-saurian anywhere who can speak the damn language without having had some sort of professional tie to its originators. It was, I was sure, as far outside Horace's ambit as the language of the angels.

But we couldn't abjure normal speech forever, and there'd be visitors; an interference net was indicated. Out of respect for Horace's capabilities, I cobbled together the most extensive job I could imagine—by hand; aid from my mechs was an unnecessary risk—and flipped the switch after ninety-seven minutes of hard labor.

"Now," Mirella said, sitting down in her chair. "I can relax. Saurian is fun, but it's hard on the system."

I nodded from my own. "Astarte Finch is dead," I said, "Horace is, at least momentarily, nullified—and we can leave that end of things to the Columbus police, I hope. Catching murderers is what they do for a living. What I do—"

"Is rescue Princesses," Mirella said. "Okay, right. So we were trying to figure out where somebody had stashed the original Amy-Robsart."

She pushed a chair-button and a Robbie came along. "Anything the Robbie knows," I said, "our eavesdropper can know. It'll transmit sight and sound from here only through the interference net—but stuff in its own records might be available in clear."

Mirella shrugged. "So let Whoever have a list of addresses," she said. "What else is it going to do for us?"

I nodded, and keyed the Robbie. A sheet of fax paper slid out of the slot, and I checked it.

FoFeality's address, and Astarte's, were both possibles, as far as location went. Sten Rann's address seemed to be the damn Palace—as I should have expected. The others seemed a little further out of range, though none was absolutely impossible.

"Suppose it *is* FoFeality," Mirella said. "So he couldn't invent a whole new thing—editing a duplicate, it is still beyond me a little—so he knows somebody who invented it, and somehow or other they got together. But it is FoFeality running the show, the other person is just an inventor."

"Very neat," I said, "and not really possible, damn it."

"Look: he knows from Totums. He kidnapped ours., He got in and poisoned things. Maybe also he shot at you with the Robbie."

"Maybe," I said, "but maybe that was our Whoever. It's a little direct for Our Horace—poisoning is more his style, though deductions about style are—"

"Teetery," Mirella said.

"Teeterboardy, anyhow," I said. "And we don't even know for sure that it was Horace who got to the damn prawns."

"He takes the Totum, he can get into the apartment, what else is there?"

I sighed. "I know," I said. "I do know. Horace is a blot on the landscape, and pinning everything on him would be a distinct pleasure. But he's been hired by somebody—why not grab the Totum on behalf of the same somebody?"

"Who also knows how to work things so we get maybe poisoned?" Mirella said. "Okay, why not? So this Whoever—not FoFeality, I will say this even if I do not want to think it—does the poisoning job once Whoever, he or she, has the Totum from FoFeality?"

"Could be," I said. "Or has Horace do the poisoning job, via the Totum—it doesn't matter much. But somebody else is running this show—and somebody else, probably, used that Robbie to shoot his bolts."

Mirella sighed. "So tell me why it can't be FoFeality," she said, and pushed the chair-button again. "But not yet. First, I need some fresh tea."

TWENTY-SEVEN

A Robbie came along. Mirella told it: "Gunpowder," and it started off again. Gunpowder is not a code for anything, it's the name of a kind of green tea. Back about five centuries—long, long before wars even got big enough to cover a planet—there was a rumor that green tea was a hallucinogen. It isn't, damn it, but it does wake up the taste buds very nicely, and Mirella's fond of the stuff. Coffee, she tells me, will eventually do me large buckets of harm somehow or other.

Well, maybe it will. Something sure as Hell will; I would enjoy living forever, but that doesn't seem to be an option. I took the opportunity to order in a pot of the dangerous stuff, and Mirella took that peaceably: she'd made her point, once, and she knew I'd heard her. From there on, she left it alone.

A very unusual person.

The Robbie came back with our orders, and when it was gone Mirella took a first sip, I took a first sip, and she said: "Okay, so tell. Why is it FoFeality can't be the one we're after? You're right, it would be a pleasure."

"Oh, we'll have *some* pleasure out of it," I said. "At the very least he stole the Totum, and sooner or later—but the rest of it: no."

"This is your theory?"

"This is solid," I said. "Suppose Horace knows our inventor. He pushes the inventor to duplicate Amy-Robsart, return the duplicate, for whatever purposes—and do all the rest of what's been happening."

"That," Mirella said, finishing the first cup, "is what I said."

"But—how does Horace know about the invention?"

She shrugged. "The inventor told him—oh."

I nodded. "Right," I said. "It has to be that the inventor told Horace about his new invention—and has never told nobody else at all."

"Maybe one other person or so, in on the plot," Mirella said.

"If he told somebody else," I said, "either the somebody else *is* in on the plot—or there would be some bustle around the Palace by now. Maybe the average Palace person can't see she's different—Amy-Robsart—or doesn't want to, but for anybody who knew duplication-and-editing was possible, every little change would be a big red flag."

"Okay," Mirella said, "so he told somebody else, who also is part of the plot. Or she."

"Which means," I said, "that the original plot belongs to the inventor. Look at it: why would he tell Horace—and maybe one other person—about the process, whatever the Hell it is—*and tell nobody else, never make it public*—unless he had something like this in mind?"

Mirella nodded slowly. "I got it, I got it," she said. "Like it, is something else, but you're right: FoFeality is not the person behind all this."

"And the addresses don't help much," I said. "Nobody's eliminated, nobody's spotlit."

"Maybe Sten Rann for the spotlight," she said.

I shook my head and poured another cup of coffee. "And he has Amy-Robsart stashed inside the damn Palace," I said, "because that's where Rann lives. I'll believe it if I have to, but I'm going to have to."

"The inventor," Mirella said. "The person running things. He has to be—or she—good enough to come up with this whole thing, editing duplicates, for God's sake. So is anybody on the list good with this sort of stuff? Maybe good enough to invent a whole new thing?"

I shrugged. "Guy Finch," I said. "He's all over everything: he works with clones, his mother just got herself killed. But—"

"But is right," Mirella said. "He's a kid, and right now, by what you tell me, he is so busted up he is not even making sense. Is anybody that good an actor? Is even an actor that good an actor, let alone a young kid likes biophysics?'"

"No," I said. "I can be fooled—but not all that easily. Guy when I last saw him was unstrung, completely. Not acting—unstrung. About the invention, though—we don't know anybody's background. Sunny Samuels might be a research genius, hiding out as a personal maid. Or it's Greensinger, or Godney Thrall. Claude Deke—"

"The least likely," Mirella said.

"And maybe, just maybe, it's somebody we haven't met yet," I said. "Unlikely, but possible."

"So why unlikely?"

"Because whoever's aiming at us—"

"So far, only at you," Mirella said.

"—has to be able to see, to aim," I said. "Has to know where we are, what we're doing."

"So he could get information," Mirella said. "Or she. From somebody we know. This is possible."

I nodded. "But not likely," I said. "If you posit enough people in on the plot, you can explain anything. But this has to work small, with as few people involved—"

"Including the universe," Mirella said.

I stared.

"Get enough people in on the plot, even the universe gets explained," she said. "It is all a con run by six hundred billion people."

"Right," I said. "But this con—this damn duplication—has a smaller cast."

All this time, you understand, the right question, and therefore the answer we needed, was sitting around positively begging to get asked. If you have that question already neatly printed up for use—and you may—all I can say is, wait around for foolish G. Knave to catch the Hell up to you. Things are simple when you get them laid out for you, all nice and neat; when you're in the middle of one event after another, Simple is not the name of the game.

Just for instance—it was about two hours after the discussion I've just told you about that two phone calls arrived, one right after the other.

The first was from Meerande Fellm, and it told me that an arrest had been made in the Astarte Finch murder case. The fellow arrested was Guy Finch.

This made no sense, as I said to Meerande in loud and simple language. She told me she knew that: "The olfactory evidence is—to the extent that it can be assayed—contradictory"—but sorting things out, she said, was going to take time.

"And we don't have time," I said. "Give this thing a while to harden, and nobody will ever be able to straighten it out."

"What thing?" she said.

I sketched out the duplication for her. "Right now, the Palace Amy-Robsart is shaky. The longer she stays around, being accepted and soaking up detail, the tougher it is going to be to blast anything loose."

Meerande made a thoughtful kind of noise. "What you tell me," she said, "is difficult to believe."

"Give it a little while," I said, "and it'll damn well be impossible to believe. And the murder has to be connected, somehow or other."

"A reasonable, if not quite a logical, necessity," she said. "Agreed."

"We'll have to do something," I said, and she told me she was doing all she could, and I agreed that more something would have to be provided from my end.

The second phone call more or less unstrung everything. It was from Sten Rann, and what Sten wanted to tell me was that a threatening letter had arrived.

TWENTY-EIGHT

It was short, and to the point—and pretty close to total non-sense.

Mirella and I headed for the Palace within seven minutes, and it only took that long because we had a brand-new lockup to take care of, and had to make sure both of us remembered to bring keys—because the Totum didn't have the new lock pattern, of course.

It took us another twenty minutes to get to a room with nobody in it but us, Sten Rann, a small, puzzled young woman with curly pinkish hair—"too shy to be a real redhead," Mirella said afterward—and the damn note. Getting to any given room in that place is not like opening your front door and heading for the den; it's just a little more like setting sail from old Liverpool (which always strikes me as the Hell of an unattractive name for anything, let alone a town) and hoping to strike the New World sooner or later. There *are* helpful servants, passersby and God knows what else—but none of them are quite helpful enough, somehow, and there is always one more staircase and two more corridors.

But we did arrive, at long, long last. Target zone was Rann's small, cluttered room, half office and half sitting-room, stuffed with dark-wood furniture, and inhabited by a fuming Sten Rann and a slightly tearful almost-redhead.

"I didn't know what it was," she was saying, in a voice that might have been very pleasant if dried out a little. "I *couldn't* know what it was."

"Of course you couldn't, Lily," Sten Rann was saying. "Nobody's blaming you."

The girl burst into tears. "I know," she said; "that's what's so awful. You're so nice about it, and it's so awful."

I broke into the domestic drama. "What is it that's awful?" I said. Mirella let the door shut behind us both with a small bang, which helped put a stop to the wailing and such.

The girl—Lily—looked around at us, her mouth open a little, and sniffled. Sten said: "Oh, it's you. Thank God. We're going to have to do something."

Everybody, it seemed, wanted something done, and everybody wanted me to be off and doing it. There's nothing like popularity, God damn it.

"Maybe we are," I said. "But what, and *about* what? On the phone you said there'd been a threatening letter, but that's all I have so far."

He sighed once, gustily, said: "Here," and handed me a sheet of thick, expensive paper. Not fax paper, but the real original stuff, looking and feeling like banknotes.

I looked around, found a small sofa, and sat down on it. Mirella got next to me, and we read the thing together.

> *Send Amy-Robsart to her father, before something bad happens. This is not a joke, and if she isn't on her way by tonight something bad* will *happen, and you wouldn't like it.*

It wasn't signed, which was not a surprise. It wasn't going to have any useful prints or heat spots on it, either, because a human being hadn't written it. That was no surprise either; few threatening letters or ransom notes these days are written by humans, whose habits of hand might betray them; Robbies have no individual hand habits to speak of, and instructing one to write a short note is not even as difficult as instructing it to walk your dog.

"Knave," Sten said after a minute or so, in a voice that was almost plaintive, "what is this all about?"

"Somebody," I said, "would either like it very much if Amy-Robsart were in Djakarta—the Emperor's still there, isn't he?"

"Some sort of local festival," Sten said. "He'll be there four days more."

I nodded. "Or," I said, "the same somebody wants Amy-Robsart away from here. I am damned if I can think of a reason why."

"Maybe he's afraid people will start noticing there's something strange about her," he said. "You noticed, didn't you? And when I heard Sunny Samuels' little fable—"

"So, just to avoid suspicion," I said, "he—or she, damn it—sends a nice threatening letter. If Amy-Robsart started acting exactly like herself two minutes from now, and Sunny Samuels told you she'd had an attack of some strange liar's disease, and cleared up every difficulty about her story—there'd still be the letter. It is not, repeat not, a sane way to calm suspicious people."

"Then what the Hell is it?" he said.

"It must mean something," I said.

Mirella looked at me. "Wait a minute," she said. "Amy-Robsart has cooled off with Guy. Now Guy is all of a sudden arrested. So does she want to look like a heartless type?"

"I see what you mean," I said, "but that makes sense only if she wrote the letter herself."

"Or if somebody who knew what she'd want wrote it," Mirella said, and I opened my mouth, shut it again and thought.

"Doesn't matter," I said at last. "We're talking as if Amy-Robsart's motives and wishes had meaning here—which they can't have. She isn't being duplicated and replaced as a service to Amy-Robsart."

"Of course not," Sten said. Mirella looked thoughtful. "But what are you talking about? What can Guy Finch have to do with this? He's—I think he's actually in custody. He can't have had a Robbie write this, not from jail."

Mirella shook he head at him. "You got it backwards," she said. "Not Guy, Amy. Look: so he's in custody, right?

"Right."

"So she stays cooled off, she doesn't go visit him, hold his hand, she is a heartless person. Right?"

"Well, if she—"

"But put her in Djakarta," Mirella said, "no way can she hold his hand. No arm is that long."

Sten nodded. "All right, I see that," he said. "But Knave said it—it doesn't make sense. Nobody did this for Amy-Robsart's comfort."

"Unless she wanted all her life to see Djakarta," Mirella said, "which is not so, because all her life what she wants is to see Tocks. Who will be anywhere off Haven IV some time during the next universe, and not before."

"Tocks?" he said. "What do Tocks have to do with it?"

I broke in. "Sten, why is Lily here? She found the letter?"

He sighed. "She delivered it," he said. I looked at the pinkish little female.

"Tell me about it," I said.

TWENTY-NINE

"I was doing my mornings," she said, after a preliminary couple of sniffles. "I do the apartments, you know? I mean not all of them, my goodness, that's a lot of people, but I do some, and today I was supposed to clean the big one."

"The Emperor's rooms," Sten put in.

The Emperor wasn't around to mess the rooms up, and there are any number of Robbies and Totums in the Palace who could be programmed for cleaning duties, but Lily was another sample of Conspicuous Conception. Everything done by humans, except where—as with the Guard—doing it with mechs was showier.

There was a little pause after Sten's helpful damn interruption, and I said: "You were cleaning the big room." Gently.

She gave me an earnest look. "I *didn't*," she said. "I was assigned. But I didn't, because of the letter."

"You found the letter in the Emperor's rooms?" I said.

Sten said: "She found it—" and I turned to him.

"Let her tell it," I said. "Works out much better that way." If Sten gave me his digest of what had happened, I'd have that; if Lily told me what she'd done, she might trip over a tiny detail Sten would miss because it obviously wasn't important.

Ninety-nine times in a hundred he'd be right, too. But the hundredth chance is what you play for, and "obviously not important" is not a phrase anywhere in my working vocabulary.

He muttered: "Sorry," and Lily looked at me with something like awe. My goodness, who was I to get such a word out of the Household Subchancellor? Then she swallowed and went back to work at telling her story.

"I found it right there, on the sofa," she said. "It's a big sofa, the green one. I told him that was where, and he knows that sofa." She indicated Sten with a nervous little gesture of her right hand.

Sten raised an eyebrow at me, and I nodded. The thing was to keep Lily feeling comfortable and conversational—as far as possible, surrounded as she was with grandees.

"The entrance to the sitting-room has a sofa facing the door," he said. "You come in, the first thing you see is the big green sofa."

"The paper was lying right on it," she said. "Kind of—kind of propped up, against the back, you know?"

"Propped up," I said. "Right you are, Lily. So you went over—"

"I went right over and picked it up," she said. "Of *course* I did. Because it didn't belong there—I mean, who could have put it there? It was litter. *Litter.* And the Emperor away, and no one else to go into his very own private rooms. So who? Of course I did."

"And you read it," I said.

She looked stricken. "I couldn't help but," she said. "It's right there, when you pick it up the words are right there."

"Of course you couldn't," I said. "And when you read it—"

I stopped to give her room, and in a second she was part-relaxed again. "I knew right away it was something strange," she said. "I mean, here is somebody telling him what to do—the Emperor, telling *him* what to do, and about his very own daughter." She made an exasperated sound. "My goodness," she said. "And him not even here, and somebody trying to give him orders. The Emperor his very own self."

"So after you read it—" I said, after a little silence.

"I took it right to Mr. Rann," she said. "Which was the right thing to do, wasn't it?" She looked not at me and not at Sten, but dead between us, and I let Sten field the ball.

"You did exactly right, Lily," he said, "and I'll see that the Housekeeper knows that you did exactly right."

And with a few small expressions of thanks here and here, and a few small queries from me that didn't give me any details that turned out useful—I found out that the sofa was covered in a green nubbly Egyptian cotton, and had to be kept just so, because it was so noticeable—Lily went out, and left the three of us there silent: me, Sten and the damn note.

A minute went by, which is a long time. Then Sten said: "Well?"

"Of course, it wasn't addressed to the Emperor," I said.

"It wasn't addressed to *any* damned body," he said. "Might have been meant for me, for Security, for the Samuels woman—a hundred others round here, take your pick."

"That," I said, "is the idea. It wasn't addressed at all—it

was meant for the Palace itself, in a way. Not for any specific person—for whoever in the Palace had the power to do what it says has to be done."

"Just dropped on a sofa in an empty room?" Sten said.

"It was efficient, wasn't it?" I said. "The rooms get cleaned whether the Emperor's at home or not, and that green sofa must be a lovely frame for a sheet of stiff, white paper. Whoever came in to do the work would have seen the note right off—and whoever saw it would read it, and there you are. It'd get to somebody in authority pretty damn fast—as it did."

"So it was left by someone who knew Palace routine," he said.

"We can do better than that," I said. "It was left by somebody who could get into the Emperor's private rooms to leave it. That can't be an immense list of people, can it?"

Immense, unfortunately, was one good word for the size of the list: there were, of course, one Hell of a lot of Palace servants and Palace officials, and any of them might have wandered in.

"Not much further," he said, "or you get down to only twenty or thirty people. but that's the entrance room, really, and anybody who might have business there—from cleaning staff to a Cabinet member—my God, we're not limited to the Palace, Knave."

"No, the whole Dichtung would have entry," I said, "not to mention the High Court. But we can cross off that end of the list fast."

"How? Question the whole Dichtung—four hundred and thirty members? And the seven on the Court—"

"No need," I said "Ask around here—ask who's seen one of them in the last twenty-four hours."

He thought for about a second. "Oh."

"Right," I said. "No reason for any of them to come into the Palace, with the Emperor away—unless there's something special about somebody—"

He thought about that. "Drang Grube—he's member for Outer Mining Interests—Grube's friendly with one of the Household secretaries, woman named Roebuck. Rita Roebuck. He might—"

"So ask Roebuck," I said. "But the answer will be no. This

has to be connected with everything else that's been happening."

"My God, I should think so," he said.

"So it'll be people already connected with that," I said. "But the big question isn't who left the note."

"No?"

"The big question," I said, "is, who the Hell wants Amy-Robsart sent to Djakarta—and why."

THIRTY

"To get her out of the way, nobody should notice the changes," Mirella said when I got back to our place—with the note, nicely bagged in clear pastic. The odds on finding any traces of anything beyond ambient dust were a million to one, but why not play it safe?

"Nice idea, but about four days late," I said. She nodded.

"When you're right, you're right," she said. "Anybody wanted to do that, it would be done four days ago. Anyhow three."

"Three," I said. "Right. After the changes began to show up for real, and our Whoever knew he was working with a shaky situation."

"And if the note gets dropped three days ago—"

"It gets found two days ago," I said. "Right. No, whatever the motive is, it isn't to hide the changes."

Mirella poured herself a second cup of tea. "There are people," she said, "think tea happens by the cup. Hard to believe, but there are some. Tea happens by the pot, a cup at a time." She swallowed. "Don't mind me," she said. "Talking helps me think, no matter about what."

"I know," I said. "But there are other motives."

"Sure there are. Somebody has something set up for her in Djakarta. Somebody has her rigged to do something or say something in Djakarta, while the Emperor's still there."

"Somebody's got her rigged to explode when she gets within three feet of the Emperor," I said. Mirella stared at me.

"This could happen?"

I shook my head. "Simpler to toss a bomb," I said. "To duplicate an entire person, in order to have her walk up to another person and explode, seems like a little too much work."

"Sure," she said. "Build a Robbie instead, make it look like Amy-Robsart—who will question? Get it close enough, bang."

"Who knows?" I said. "It might even work—if that's what you're after. No, this has to have a better motive."

"Something she has to do in Djakarta."

"Or something she has to avoid doing here," I said. "God damn it, this makes no sense whatever."

"No sense yet, that much I can see," Mirella said. "Why no sense whatever?"

"You create a duplicate Amy-Robsart," I said. "You edit the original, for your own purposes. You drop her into the Palace—and then you toss in a threat, to move her to Djakarta."

"You said it days ago," Mirella told me. "A new idea, you have to try it out, maybe something will go wrong. You got plans for Djakarta, you try out your Amy-Robsart copy first someplace else. It is okay, then you get her in position."

"That," I said, "is a perfect description of why this makes no sense."

Mirella gave me her sigh. "Okay," she said. "I am a simple barefoot police person. Explain."

"Easy," I said. "You want to try out your duplicate—so you drop her in front of the toughest audience known, right here in the Palace where everybody watches everything. Where there are people like Sten Rann, who know her all her life, maybe better than a preoccupied Emperor and companion are going to. It's a tryout with a tougher audience than the one for opening night."

Mirella nodded. "When you're right—" she said.

"There's more," I said. "You edit your copy, for your own purposes. But you don't give her any push toward going to Dja-karta—and there must be fifty possible motives, easy to supply."

"She is maybe lonely for her family," Mirella said.

"Or she feels left out, or she has something she just has to tell her father, in person, right away—or any number of other notions. My God, there's no shortage. And if you can edit the copy—"

"You can put one in," Mirella said. "Like a what-is-it—a postal hypno."

"Post-hypnotic," I said. "When you hear the word *fricative*, you will feel like going to Djakarta."

"Fricative?"

"It means something about producing a sound with your tongue," I said.

"Disappointing," she said. "It sounds dirty, but no." She shrugged. "But nobody put in a key like that."

"Our Whoever—who is bright and fast, on all the evidence—left it to a threatening note, sure to arouse *some* kind of suspicion." I gave Mirella a sigh of my own, less operatic than hers. "I said it: no sense whatever."

Mirella nodded, and poured a new cup of tea. "You lay it out clear," she said, "I see why it is full of mud. But senseless, it can't be."

"No," I said. "Somehow, this shakes down into a perfectly sensible set of actions. Criminal, dangerous, confusing—but sensible."

"What we got," she said, "is more questions."

I nodded. "And not an answer in sight."

And no time to sit and think about answers, either. Guy Finch was in jail, and we damn well had to go and try getting him out of jail.

"So why?" Mirella said when I brought it up, a minute or so later. "In jail he is nice and peaceful, he is not in danger, and he will stay put. What's the harm, we leave him there a while?"

"First of all, he's panicked," I said. "Calm and peaceful can't describe him—he got shoved into a cell, where he can't find out anything about anything except what time lunch gets sent in—either he's climbing the walls, or he's edging right into catatonia."

"So, very sad for Guy," she said. "But why is this our business, all of a sudden? I would say help him, but we got a lot to do."

"Second—wait a minute—second, he didn't do it," I said. "Somebody else did; let's get things arranged right."

"Which is neat, but not urgent," she said. "The question is—"

"Why is it our business?" I said. "Because, damn it, if anybody can help me with the whole business of How—figuring out what this process of duplicating people with changes actually is, and how it's done—Guy is it. And if I have to ask him any questions at all, let alone complicated ones, it'd be nice if he were in shape to understand simple sentences, and just possibly arrange to reply."

Mirella sighed again. "When you're right," she said, "who can argue?"

THIRTY-ONE

I am not—contrary to a few rather nasty rumors—an expert on police stations throughout the Comity. I have seen some, on a small variety of planets and for a small variety of reasons, but, as it happens, I'd never seen an Earth police station before. I still don't know whether the one I saw in Columbus is typical of the whole planet—it may be some sort of Imperial specialty—but it wasn't much like any of the others I'd seen.

There are three basic functions for any police station, anywhere; you need a place for police officers to meet and carry on their business, you need a place to stash suspects and criminal types while the business is going on, and you need a place where members of the local public can come and ask questions. All three of those places were present in the large Columbus station I went to, where Guy Finch was languishing, but they were almost dwarfed by a fourth function.

The building itself—and let's begin right there—was painted a bright, cheery green, with thin yellow stripes here and there to accent a window or a door. It looked as if it had been polished every day for thirty years. Over the door—which was metal painted to look like expensive wood—there was a sign, in yellow on a black background. I think the colors were a mistake—black is not a cheery color, for the most part, and the combination was bound to make Earth locals think of bees, which are busy little insects that sting you, painfully, on virtually no provocation. But, in a way, the whole sign was a mistake.

It said: WELCOME TO YOUR POLICE FACILITY—in the largest letters you can imagine. Under that, in letters smaller only by comparison, it said: YOUR TAX DOLLARS AT WORK.

No matter why I come to a police station, I do not want to be welcomed brightly and cheerily. I may be a police officer, doing the daily tough work. I may be a criminal or a suspect, dragged to the place by officers and wanting nothing so much as to be somewhere else—anywhere else. I might be a local citizen, there to ask a question of some kind—and the kind of question one goes to a police station to ask is not likely to give anybody the room to feel cheery.

All right. I went up four steps to the painted door and pushed on it. It swung open with a small and apologetic creak. Mirella was right behind me, muttering under her breath, and we got inside and the door swung shut behind us.

We were in a large box of a room, with a raised desk on the left and two sets of stairs going off at angles ahead of us. Chairs and benches littered the place, and a few local citizens, or police in plain clothes—almost offensively plain clothes—were lounging around on this or that bench. Mirella took one comprehensive look at the place and said:

"Welcome. Who welcomes to a station house? Better a sign says Beware." Then she nudged me. "Must be the duty officer over there," she said, and indicated the desk.

"This isn't your planet," I said. "Let me handle it, right?"

"Feel free," she said. "Welcome, for God's sake. I would not handle with long, long tongs."

She walked behind me, quietly, as I headed for the woman at the desk. The woman was a large, square person with a high crown of yellow-white hair twisted all around her head, and a pair of narrow, metal-rimmed spectacles. She wore what I assumed was the local uniform—a little gaudy for my taste, with fringed gold epaulets, in bright yellow, with black collar, edgings and cuffs. She looked at me with as sad a face as I remember seeing anywhere, and said in an equally sad monotone:

"Welcome to your local police facility. Every officer in this district is anxious and eager to serve you. How may I be of help?"

I felt as if I were talking to a Totum that had had some deep personal tragedy. "My name is Gerald Knave," I said. "There's a man named Guy Finch being held here, and my wife and I would like—"

"Oh," she said, in the same mournful hoot. "The murderer."

I took a breath. "Well, that isn't quite a certainty," I said. "Not yet. We'd like to see him. And talk with him," I added.

She looked down at me from the desk height. Her voice didn't change. "Why?" she said.

Mirella made a small sound. I said: "He's a friend. We'd like to find out a little about his case—what's being done, what he's accused of and why, all of that. He isn't really a murderer, you see, and we'd like—"

"We can tell you all of that," the woman said. "He's accused of murder, and for good reason too. What's being done is, we're building up the case against him right now. Anything else you want to know?"

I have no idea what I would have said just then. Mirella saved me the trouble of finding it. She took a step and a half sidewise, which put her next to me, and said, in a tone of puzzled disbelief:

"You're a police officer? A real police officer?"

The woman stared down. As she moved her head to focus on Mirella, who is a lot shorter than I am, the yellow-white hair structure wobbled. "I," she said—and ice came into her voice—"am Draeca Garnet, a Sergeant of Police for this district. Who the Hell are you?"

"I the Hell am Mrs. Mirella Knave," Mirella said, "and I am a Lance-Corporal of Police in City Two on Ravenal." The woman looked very faintly struck—Ravenal is one of those names that impresses people, about the way, say, M. I. T. used to long ago, or the Institute for Advanced Students at Princeton—and Mirella took a breath and added: "Lance-Corporal corresponds to your Captain."

This was a flat lie, and I am not sure Sergeant Garnet bought it—but she didn't *not* buy it, either. "We have, as you may know—" she began, but Mirella, who had the edge, wasn't about to give it up by letting her finish.

"A working relationship with the Ravenal authorities," she said. "I know Not that there's much use for it—a few Earth fugitives get returned, maybe. We don't let criminals off Ravenal, not in my time."

"Is there some connection with Ravenal in this case?" Garnet said. "I will be frank, with a fellow officer: we have not turned up any such connection. Of course, we've only had a few hours—"

"Time enough if there was one," Mirella said flatly, "and there isn't. But we're interested in the case, Sergeant. There may be—similarities to other recent murders—"

"On Ravenal?" Garnet said. I'd been completely forgotten, and glad to stay that way; it may not have been Mirella's planet, but it was sure as Hell her profession.

"Might be the case," Mirella said. "It's not something we want to talk about a lot." She gave Garnet a smile I recognized as one of mine: friendly, casual and fake. "You know how it is," she said.

Garnet nodded. "And you want—"

"To see this Finch," Mirella said. "Private. Question him a little. Maybe a lot."

"With a stenograph running—" Garnet said.

"No records," Mirella said. "Not right now, no." She took another breath. "Look, you want this all through channels, I'll get the Ambassador to come over," she said. "But it takes time and it means you get tied up as liaison."

"Well—"

"Believe it," Mirella said, "you do not want to be liaison. Like a translator—nothing to do but pass notes, but something happens, who gets blamed? The liaison. To a nice officer, this shouldn't happen, so why should it?"

"Well—" Garnet said again.

"Do it all quiet," Mirella said, "and nobody gets blamed. Because who would know but you and me, Sergeant?"

"We can't simply—"

"I tell you, Captain to Sergeant—Lance to Sergeant—it is very simple. In City Two we had a case like this, needed to be done quiet. My officers handled it that way—quiet. Got commendations out of it. City Two, that's on Ravenal."

"Well, perhaps—" Garnet said.

Mirella nodded. Decisively. "Good," she said. "No escort— just tell us how to go where, we'll explore."

"But perhaps if—"

"No escort," Mirella said again. "Quiet, that's the way, believe it. I will report to you back, myself personally." Garnet looked faintly indecisive; the hair wobbled again. Mirella said suddenly: "I tell you what. You got a track light here? Must have, everybody does. Strap one on me, you can't lose me. I go see Finch, I come back—I go any other place, you know from the track. It is still quiet, but now also it is safe."

Garnet hesitated about two seconds, produced a strap-on, keyed it and watched as Mirella fastened it onto her wrist. The two of them keyed it to her pulse—now, if she unstrapped it and left it somewhere an alarm would now go off—and Mirella said:

"Fine. Good job, Sergeant. Now, where is it we go?"

"Both of you want to—"

"He's with me," Mirella said, with an offhand gesture toward the invisible man.

THIRTY-TWO

Halfway up the right-hand stairway, Mirella turned to me. "Idiots, you have to give idiot speeches to," she said. "Welcome, for God's sake."

"You did a beautiful job," I said, climbing behind her.

"Easy," she said. "Idiots we have in City Two, who can be immune? But this much sense we got—we do not put them in charge of anything. Remember Paolo?"

I nodded. "Your partner, when I met you," I said.

"Partner," she said. "A baby I had to sit on. So I looked at this Garnet, I pretended she was Paolo."

"Well, congratulations," I said. "It worked."

"So *something* worked," Mirella said. ""Let us only hope, the next something will not only work, but also be more important."

I nodded again, as we reached the landing. We headed left, into a long corridor. Four feet or so further along, there was a gate, with a Robbie standing by it.

Mirella looked at the Robbie, disapprovingly. "Machines you do not use for guard duty," she said. "Machines can be fixed even easier than people, and cheaper too." She waited a second, and said: "Maybe I should give it a password, which the Garnet idiot forgot to tell me."

Another second went by, and then the Robbie creaked into action. Up here where visitors didn't usually go, nobody was wasting money on signs, on glitter—or on proper maintenance either. But that was their worry, thank God, and not ours. The Robbie unlocked the gate, and slid back to let us through. Behind us, it swung the gate shut again, without relocking it.

"Careless, and not good," Mirella said, "but no complaint. He locked it again, maybe he would forget how to unlock. Welcome."

The corridor went on for a few feet, and on the right-hand side there was a barred cell door. As we got there, a very tired voice said: "It isn't locked. Come on in."

The lighting was miserable—it was as dim up there as if we were all in a 3V horror show waiting for a monster to turn up. But the door was visible; I tried it and it swung a little. I pushed harder and it creaked slowly open, and we went in, to Guy Finch's cell.

There was a cot, a single chair, a sink, a broken-down toilet, and a single dim light source in the ceiling. The light source was shielded with a wire basket, which made no sense that I could see, as the chair and cot were not movable. Guy was standing by the cot, and gave us a shaky little gesture of welcome.

I said hello, and sat down on the cot; Mirella took the chair when Guy gestured at it, and Guy paced to the open door of the cell, turned and looked at us, bracing himself against the bars. He looked better than I'd thought he might be—confused and shaken, but, for a change, conscious of his surroundings.

"Nice of you to come and visit," he said, his voice still tired and dragging a little.

"I have to say, sorry," Mirella said. "We should maybe bring cookies. Or a bottle of wine. Anyhow, something, we come to a housewarming."

"Cell-warming," I said, and Mirella shook hr head.

"So why remind anybody?" she said. "Cell warming sounds like something Guy does with his work. Housewarming is better."

Guy laughed—just a little at first, but Mirella cocked her head at him and the laugh became a real one. I made a note never to visit anybody in jail without bringing her along.

"I don't actually warm cells," he said. "Though there is heat involved—has to be."

"Necessary by-product of damn near anything," I said, and he nodded.

"Even a change in electron orbits releases—well, heat," he said. "Increase of particle speed, translated as heat." He shook his head. "But you didn't come here to discuss particle physics," he said. "You—why *did* you come here?"

Mirella was on a roll, and I let her have it. "First," she said, "you are in a cell, it is not a nice place to be. So maybe a visit helps a little."

"It does," he said. "I can go down to the end of the corridor— well, to the gate—and look at the Robbie, but there's not much—much give-and-take about it. And—well, a couple of times somebody's come up to ask me questions, but—" He shrugged. "That isn't really very pleasant. They think—"

"They think you killed your mother," Mirella said. "A natural thing to think—crazy, but natural. She was there, you were there, so why not?" She shook her head sadly. "Much sense, these people do not have," she said. "They make do with the best they got, I guess—but they can use some help, right?"

"Right," Guy said. "It's ridiculous—to think I would k— kill—I would—"

And he sat down and started to cry. He didn't get to the cot, he just sat in the cell doorway, his head in his hands. I made the beginning of a move toward him and Mirella stopped me with a gesture. A minute or so went by. Then Mirella got up and went to the cell door. She murmured: "Excuse it, okay?" and Guy edged out of her way, and she started out.

"Don't leave," Guy said in a muffled voice. Mirella had remembered, as I had, that Guy was going to be more comfortable without females around—and, while I'd been thinking of a way to arrange that, she'd found one. But apparently she didn't count as female—or else she was being some kind of maternal figure for him.

Mirella nodded. "Okay," she said. "So we'll all sit around and talk for a while."

Guy stood up, leaning against the open door. "About what?" he said.

"Anything," Mirella said. "Why not a little quiet talking? Clone states, we could start there, nice and harmless."

Guy hesitated for a second, and then shrugged. "Okay," he said. "Why not?" And he was looking a little more relaxed.

"Me," Mirella said, "I have no idea even what they are."

"It's—an odd place for a seminar," Guy said. The ghost of a smile flickered on his face and was gone. The tears had dried.

"Place doesn't matter," I said. "Call it—a virtual lecture-hall. I got interested in what you were saying—when you visited. How cloning people was impossible, because of personality changes."

He frowned at me, and then looked back at Mirella, sitting in the chair. "Not impossible," he said. "It is possible to create an exact copy—though not precisely a clone."

"A duplicate," I said.

"Certainly a duplicate," he said. "The key lies in Bose-Einstein pairs."

I nodded. Mirella said: "Bose and Einstein. Einstein I know, and Bose was also back then. He made sound amplifiers."

Guy smiled again, a real smile. "Not the same Bose," he said. "This one was a physicist. And what they found—well, start with electrons."

"Always a good place," Mirella said. "Start small, how can you go wrong?"

"Electrons exist in orbits," Guy said. "Like planets—only there can be more than one electron in the same orbit. Shells, we call them."

"Electron shells," Mirella said. "Going around and around. This, I have heard of a little."

"But there's a limit to how many electrons are in a given orbit," Guy said. I was nodding.

"And they change shells—orbits—depending on the state of the atom involved."

"Very, very roughly, yes," Guy said. He was, thank God, back in the lecture hall, "Except—sometimes that isn't quite so."

"The sometimes is Bose," Mirella said. "Also Einstein. Right?"

"Under certain conditions—the Ancients used low temperatures, but we have fields that can do the same thing—electrons can superpose. Exist in the same orbit. Double up, so to speak—where an electron shell might have eight electrons in it, under Bose-Einstein conditions it might have sixteen."

"So you have two atoms in one jumper," Mirella said. "Gets crowded."

"There's space for the additions," Guy said. "So to speak. But what we've begun to discover—and this is the exciting part—is that Bose-Einstein particles—duplication of state and shell—can give rise to BCE particles."

I'd read a little about that, somewhere—it was the ghost of my notion for duplication. But I let Guy tell it; the little I knew, or thought I knew, was nothing like enough.

"Even for a particle," Mirella said, "BCE is a funny name. Something happened to A and D?"

"Bose, Chandrasekhar and Einstein," Guy said. "Sometimes Ancient physicists used their initials—there's an ABC reaction, for instance, for three people named Alpher, Bethe and Gamow." He was in full swing. "You see, alpha, beta and gamma are the first three letters of the Greek alphabet, so they thought their names, put together that way, made a good pun."

"And BCE is the first letters of something?" Mirella said. "Or else I am maybe confused."

"Just their names," Guy said. "Bose—not the one who made amplifiers—Chandrasekhar—Knave here probably knows that name—"

"Chandrasekhar's Limit," I said automatically. "Astrophysics."

"Right," Guy said. "And Einstein. They made a joint discovery, away back then—even before space travel—that, if something is done to an electron right here—"

"Right here where we are?" Mirella said.

"Might as well be," Guy said. "Any electron. If its position or velocity is changed—or if an outside force changes its state, say—the same thing happens to *another* electron, somewhere else."

I nodded. "A kind of reflection," I said.

"Under certain conditions," Guy said, "if you use an outside force on an electron here, you can *create* an electron somewhere else."

"Hey," Mirella said. "Where?"

Guy smiled at her. The lecturer looking at a good student. "That," he said, "was the problem. There was no way to tell where the new electron would turn up. Next door—or in orbit around Sirius—or in the Horsehead Nebula. Another electron would appear—but there was no way to tell where."

Mirella shook her head. "This they found out, electrons around Sirius or someplace," she said, "with no space travel to go and maybe see for themselves?"

"It was a mathematical inference then, really," Guy said. "But we've been able—this is the exciting part, really—we've been able to confirm it experimentally."

I looked at him, making it as open and friendly a baffled stare as I could manage. "Wait a minute," I said. "You mean you've been able to look for—and find—*one electron*, created when you fiddled with another electron—one electron, orbiting Sirius or, my God, even in the next room?"

Guy smiled at me. The lecturer preparing the surprise that would blow his little class of listeners right out of the water. "Well, we were able to simplify the problem," he said mildly. "You see, we now know where the BCE particle—the new electron—will appear. We can control it."

THIRTY-THREE

I did my very best to look astonished, and Mirella didn't have to try. But it had been a deductive necessity: if you were going to duplicate people, you needed to be able to create electrons—not to mention neutrons, protons and a barrelful of all sorts of particles—and, obviously, you needed to be able to predict where they would turn up.

I let Mirella say it—her honest surprise would be more persuasive than my acting, however good my acting was. "That's impossible," she said. "If you can do that—"

"Clone states," he said. "We can create clone states—whole new copies of actual artifacts."

"What kind of objects?" I said. "People are out, we know that—you can't duplicate people because of the uncertainty factor. But—"

"Yes," he said, just a little too quickly, "people are out." He paused. "Lab objects, of course," he went on. "Cubes of metal, simple elements. But you can see how exciting the vista is."

"I certainly can," Mirella said. And we went on talking for a while, and we left Guy Finch acting more relaxed and more cheerful than he'd been doing when we got there. Our good deed for the day. And on the way home by local taxi, Mirella said:

"He is a nice young fellow. I will not believe it. That a nice young fellow turns into what's-his-name—who was it murdered his mother and married his father?"

"Oedipus," I said, and you've got it backward, but never mind. What else is there to think? You heard him about duplicating people.'"

"Too fast, too flat," she agreed. "A person tells me, like that, the sun is up, I look around for the night sky. But—Jerry, it is easier to believe Claude Deke."

"And you didn't see him right after the body got discovered—right after he called me," I aid. "If he's that good an actor, he should be starring in—wait a minute. He can't be that good an actor."

"Nobody is," Mirella said.

"Meerande would have noticed," I said. "The smells wouldn't have added up the way they did. Anxiety, she said, great anxiety. Not much else—not rage, for instance."

"You told me," Mirella told me. "Interesting."

"But if Guy Finch—"

"Some anxiety anyhow," she said. "You kill somebody, you are going to be anxious. Who knows for certain what you left behind, somebody might pick up? But not the picture you gave me. And the no rage—"

"Hit the woman once, maybe twice," I said, "and all we can see is, you wanted to hurt her or kill her. Beat her as thoroughly as Astarte Finch was beaten—hit again and again—you have to see rage in the picture. But there wasn't any."

"So there are other reasons," Mirella said. "Back in City Two we had an idiot—this goes back, my second year on the Force there—shot another idiot. So he wanted to hide the shot."

"Don't tell me," I said.

Mirella nodded. The taxi stopped, I put my card in the slot and took it out diminished by a couple of dollars, and we went upstairs. I opened the door, and Mirella set a Robbie to getting some coffee and a pot of tea. We sat down to wait for it, and she said: "Don't tell you, but that's how it was. He beat the body with an old stick, some kind. Figured it would pass for a death by beating, nobody would bother to look."

I nodded. "But bothering to look—"

"Is what police people do," Mirella said, and poured out the first cup of tea. I took a swallow of coffee—the Tock blend; I'd taken a little more than a pound out of ship's store for myself, while I was at it. "Bullet still in the body, even."

I swallowed more coffee. "But that wasn't the motive here," I said. "Nobody's mentioned another cause of death, and there's been time for a good preliminary look."

"So where there is one motive, there are six," Mirella said. "And one more thing to say—anybody kills another person, he has to be crazy. Or she. Could be there are reasons for the crazy, but you kill somebody, you are not right in the head."

I nodded again. "I've heard you say that before," I said.

"Any time somebody kills somebody," Mirella said, "you will hear me with it. But take a minute and look. Guy Finch is crazy?"

"Anybody can be crazy," I said. "But crazy like that—I can't believe it either. Which leaves us only one place to go."

Mirella poured a second cup of tea. "We got two different things going on here," she said. "Stitched up to look like one—"

"Maybe stitched up by accident," I said.

"Maybe anything," she said, "but two things. One is Amy-Robsart. And on that, it is Guy Finch, no second choice."

"And the other," I said, "is Astarte Finch. Which is somebody—but not Guy."

There was a little silence. Then Mirella said: "You know, you come to something like this, it should make things simple. But look: everything has got even more complicated."

"I know," I said.

"Because somebody rigs our Totum, somebody tries to poison us—somebody takes two shots at you—and who is that? The Amy-Robsart person or the Astarte Finch person? Or people."

I sighed, finished the coffee and punched the chair button for a second cup. "I am damned if I know," I said.

THIRTY-FOUR

But there were, of course, other questions. Mirella brought up the first one.

"Guy Finch is a bright kid," she said.

"Right."

"And a bright kid who is duplicating a human being—with changes, and nobody has got an explanation for the changes yet—he knows there is going to be suspicious people around."

"Right," I said again.

"And he knows, if there is suspicious people, you and me are going to be at least two of them, if not six or maybe eleven."

I nodded. "So," I said, "why did he feed us that lecture?"

Mirella finished the second cup and poured a third. "He did say people is impossible," she offered.

"And he wasn't convincing, and he never had to open the bag at all. Pasting that little label on it is useless—we'd go look."

"Maybe for anybody else, people is impossible," she said. "For him, maybe he has a way."

"So he puts up road signs, pointing to Guy Finch and nobody else?"

She nodded and took a sip. "Right," she said. "He never so much as mentioned another name."

"Einstein, Bose and Chandrasekhar," I said. "Not available as suspects."

"He opened it up for us," Mirella said. "He didn't have to do that."

"So why did he?" I said, and she looked at me.

"Maybe," she said, "because he wants us to know."

Which opened up several more boxes. After a while, Mirella said: "You know, this is funny. This is for real very funny."

I sighed. "Tell me why," I said.

She gave me a grin over her fourth cup. "All this started, seems weeks and weeks ago but only days—we were worried about Amy-Robsart. Now Amy-Robsart is the only thing *not* to worry for."

"I wouldn't go that far," I said, and she nodded and finished off the cup. I finished my second cup of coffee and spelled it all out. "Accidents can happen," I said. "And somehow or other, everything is still connected. We said—stitched together by coincidence."

"You said," Mirella told me. "I said—maybe anything."

"All right. But it wasn't accident. When we started looking, everything else started—the shot bolts, the poison try—"

"And since Astarte Finch is dead," she said, "there has not been even a ghost, one more try."

"No, since before that," I said. "Since I told Horace FoFeality we knew about the kidnapped Totum."

"So," she said. "FoFeality got nervous, and quit trying—"

"Maybe," I said. "And maybe almost anything else. If there's another try tomorrow—"

"Why wait?" Mirella said. "This is a fast worker, this Whoever. Why not today? We have been in and out, we have been in a public taxi, we have come back, and what? Nothing."

"Maybe he couldn't rig anything," I said uneasily.

"Or she," Mirella said. "And this one rigs a Robbie, rigs our Totum, poisons *your prawns*—he can't find something else?"

"Maybe," I said slowly, "he's been busy."

"Or she," Mirella said. "That sounds like a possible. Busy killing Astarte Finch."

"With a blood-spattered Totum—which didn't do the murder all by itself, for God's sake—and some fax paper." I sighed again and pushed the chair button.

"Tea you can drink by the pot," Mirella said. "Drink coffee by the pot, you will sleep maybe next Thursday."

"That fax paper still worries me," I said. "What was it doing there—and why wasn't it there any more?"

"It was the murder weapon," Mirella said, "so the killer had to take it away."

I waved off the Robbie: Cancel. It turned and went out again. "You beat somebody to death with fax paper," I said, "you do it with a couple of reams of the stuff. And you take the weapon away in a wheelbarrow."

"A couple reams, I can carry myself," Mirella said.

"It's still silly," I said.

"Sherlock Holmes," she said. "You even told it to me. Take all the silly things, throw out the ones don't work, what's left works."

"Close enough," I said. "But the fax paper—if it wasn't the murder weapon—and a couple of reams of paper to beat somebody to death with is one of the silly things that gets thrown out—"

"Probably," Mirella said with regret. "Be a first, though."

"For the entire history of the human race, I think," I said. "Anyhow, if that isn't so—what was the fax paper doing there?"

"So she was alone in her room," Mirella said. "Maybe a little light reading."

"And the killer took it away with him," I said. "Or her."

"We are going to have to find it," she said. "Then we'll know why and what."

"Unless the killer burned it," I said, and then: "This isn't getting us anywhere."

"You got better ideas?" she said, and the noise started.

I have a good, solid front door—but there's a limit to door strength. Whoever, or whatever, was pounding on mine sounded as if it would discover that limit, and surpass it, within minutes, possibly within seconds. Mirella raised an eyebrow.

"You expecting—" Pound. "—somebody?" she said.

"Nobody could be expecting that," I said, between more pounds. Mirella thought for a second.

"Open it?" she said.

"Doesn't sound friendly."

"So shield up first. It is a try, let it be a try, we find out some more."

THIRTY-FIVE

The damn pounding stopped—for about ninety seconds. Then it started up again, if possible louder. The door wasn't giving way, but ithe noise sounded to me as if it would start shaking in another few seconds, and after that a collapse was distinctly possible.

We shielded up fast—a couple of field arrangements, keyed to belts I found in the front-hall table drawer: a Survivor is ready for any emergency, according to the 3V—which is not true, but works fairly well for the emergencies you happen to think of. The pounding, restarted, had gone on for about fifty seconds when I threw the latch and opened the door, stepping well back and to the right. Mirella was directly behind me after I'd moved.

That left the center and the left of the hallway for the Robbie to wheel itself in. It wasn't any larger or more massive than the usual breed, a spindly sort of five-foot human shape, in dully shining metal, with a large head and chest. Could it have done all that pounding?

Probably not, and I cursed under my breath. The Robbie wheeled, looked at the hallway, located the two of us standing there—doing nothing much except looking back at it: if you're going to be a target, be a helpful one—and backed so that it was standing against the left-hand wall, facing us and the hallway table on the right-hand side. A couple of seconds passed by in silence.

I've got the only apartment on the floor, so there were no neighborly heads poking out of doorways to see what the Hell the hooraw had been—in any case, as I've said, I took care when I first moved in to ensure non-inquisitive neighbors, and the record has been kept through the years.

I fully expected the Robbie to pull a gun—or just maybe a couple of reams of fax paper—from a holding cavity. If it did, I was prepared; my own slug gun will shoot through my own field, it was well tucked away, and I'm a fast draw. I suppose Mirella had an equally prepared weapon or two stashed somewhere about her person, though I hadn't seen her go for one, having been busy fishing out the field belts.

Then—a second or so having gone by in that frozen silence—the Robbie surprised the Hell out of me.

"I might have been a bomb," it said, "of virtually any size and power. Please take note." The voice was not familiar, and might have been mechanical—a voder of some kind.

Robbies (as I've said) don't talk.

Open-mouthed and silent, we watched the thing wheel itself around, find the open door, and scurry right the Hell out of it, and out of our lives. I shut the door without even thinking about it, and it was something like two minutes later when it occurred to me that the sensible thing would have been to trap the Robbie—maybe our Totum could have managed that, with help from the staff and from us—and, just maybe, find out something about who had sent it.

By then, of course, it had found the elevator, descended and gotten itself nicely lost in local traffic.

Well, maybe we couldn't have captured it, anyhow—we didn't have a handy trap rigged, as FoFeality had had for our Totum.

And it had left something behind. A small, hairy bundle lay on my doorstep, unnoticed in all the hooraw. I went over to it.

It was a dog, a wire-haired variety. Light-brown, with white spots in a pattern I thought I recognized.

Oh, God.

Mirella said: "Recorded program."

"Both of them," I said, having recovered my wits while staring at Drone, Amy-Robsart's pet. "The pounding, and the speech. Pounding keyed to finding the right door, speech keyed to finding the right people." Drone, or of course a duplicate.

""Maybe just the right person," she said. "Only one of us is home, that would maybe do."

"Either way," I said. "But, my God. One of the Palace Guard?"

Mirella shrugged. "Could be," she said. "But maybe not too. Tough to build response circuits into any Robbie—but this didn't have to be full response."

"Just a key program for a small recorder," I said. "It could carry the recorder and speaker in a cavity, linked to a key program set in the innards."

"Not too tough to do," Mirella said thoughtfully.

"Right," I said. "This is the first try at us that didn't need a robotics expert to manage."

"And *was* it a try?" Mirella said. "A message is not a bomb."

I picked up the dog. Mirella was eyeing it uncomfortably. "Could have been," I said. "Maybe Whoever didn't want any more innocent bystanders wiped out—a good bomb might destroy the Nieblings."

"Downstairs?" Mirella said, and I nodded. The dog moved in my arms. Sleeping, or drugged. "Nothing else, we would fall through on top, two people, a floor and a lot of hailstones. They got hail, this planet?"

"I think so," I said. "Most planets with human-type weather do, somewhere or other. Hailstones consisting of—"

"Furniture, pieces of guide wiring, walls, and who knows what," Mirella said. "Who it didn't kill, still it would damage."

I thought for half a second. "But consideration for others isn't Whoever's style."

"So he couldn't find a bomb right away," Mirella said, "and he was in a hurry. This Whoever, a fast worker, remember?"

"And an efficient one," I said. "Nobody has ever come closer. Better to assume, whatever he did, it was what he wanted to do."

"Or she," Mirella said. "Or—I am still thinking FoFeality—it. Okay," she agreed.

"He tries to kill us twice, and then he tries to warn us," I said. "This makes no sense at all." The dog yapped, twice, not loudly, and opened an eye. Mirella was resolutely ignoring it.

She frowned. "Warning shot first, then you hit. What sense hitting, and then warning?"

"Well," I said, "he didn't hit—he missed. Twice."

"You he missed twice," Mirella said. "Or it; for me FoFeality is still big. Me only once."

"Don't brood over it," I said. "But there has to be a reason. Our Whoever does what he wants to do—he misses, but not by much."

"Agreed again," Mirella said. "And just on the way—how could anybody know we are here, or even one of us is here? Lots of activity around Columbus, we might be anyplace."

"Night clubs, receptions, God knows what," I said. "Right. Lights on would be a clue, at night—but this is afternoon.

Seems later, somehow."

"A lot happens, time scrunches up," Mirella said. She kept looking at the dog.

"So it does," I said. "He had to know long enough beforehand to send the Robbie—from somewhere."

Mirella started to say something, stopped, and then shook her head. "Nothing," she said. "That's all he had to know."

"How come?"

"If nobody is here, so the Robbie does his pounding—five minutes? Eight? Who cares, we're all alone on the floor, soundproofing is good. No answer, so he turns off the record and goes away. What difference?"

"And tries again tonight," I said. "Good thinking."

"Not good enough," Mirella said. "This Whoever, takes two good shots, and then bang, a warning. Good thinking tells us why." She took a breath. "All right, I will bite," she said. "What is that thing?"

"Drone," I said. "Amy-Robsart's dog. Or a duplicate. To underline the warning, maybe. Left here—I suppose by the Robbie who came pounding. I doubt some stranger crept in, left it silently at the door, and fled."

"I do not like this," Mirella said. "Not one small tiny bit."

"It's a clue," I said. "Maybe it isn't Drone. Maybe it's a duplicate."

"With a changed personality, right?"

"Maybe," I said. "Maybe this is a message from the kidnapper. The inventor. I really did it, he's saying. Any false moves, and the original Amy-Robsart will be in even more danger."

"He sends this message to us?" Mirella said. "Not to the Palace?"

"Yes," I said. "That does look strange, doesn't it?

THIRTY-SIX

"Okay," Mirella said, a minute later. "So what do we do with it?"

"We hang on to it," I said. "In case it's the original—or in case it's not. And we—"

"I am not big on pets," Mirella said. "For other people, fine. For me, no. Not even a fish."

"I know," I said. "It'll only be until we can—"

"Figure all this out, sure," Mirella said. "And meanwhile, who walks, who feeds, who takes care?"

"It's programmable," I said. "The Totum and the Robbies have pet-program links built in, they always do. I can punch in the specs, and you won't be bothered."

"Just the sight of it, I am already bothered," Mirella said. "But who could kill such a little hairy thing? It is here, here it will be. For a while only."

"Promise," I said, and a verse popped into my head, out of the stew of Classical learning that's still stuck away in there someplace. I recited it.

"I am His Highness' dog at Kew. Pray tell me, Sir, whose dog are you?"

Mirella stared. "What is that?"

"Poem for a dog-collar," I said, "on a real dog. Written by Alexander Poop, or Pope. I prefer Poop, it's appropriate. Eighteenth century."

"Kew is a placc?"

"Where a local Highness lived, I suppose, who had a dog," I said. "Forget it." I put the dog down. It stood shakily, and then more steadily, and looked up at me. It yapped experimentally. I said: "Good dog," and Mirella said:

"How do you know? Maybe bad dog, but here we are stuck with it."

"And with a lot of other things," I said. "A whole nest of them." Which we discussed—after I made one fast, cautious phone call.

The Palace. And what we had, it seemed, was Drone II: Drone I was still yapping its little head off in the Palace.

All right, discussion. For instance:

1. If Guy Finch had been involved in kidnapping and replacing Amy-Robsart Berringer—first of all, why? They'd had a romance going, and the new Amy-Robsart had cooled off suddenly—but it seemed like a very hard way to rid yourself of a romantic encumbrance, no matter how scientifically you wanted to go about doing that.
2. On the same assumption, why had Guy fed us all the data that made his involvement almost a certainty?
3. How had Astarte Finch been killed, by whom, and how was fax paper involved?
4. Who was taking pot shots at the Knaves, and why? To keep us from finding out about Amy-Robsart? The timing made that a near-certainty, but it also made no sense: see 2.
5. And, after two good shots at us (all right, one at us, one at me), why a warning?
6. And just to make an even half-dozen—how was all this connected? It had to be—again, the timing showed it. But none of the connections were—never mind visible—really, solidly imaginable.

It was a lovely list. Not one bit of it made any recognizable sense at all.

Sooner or later, I told myself, it would. This was just as small a comfort as it always is.

There were, of course, other things to worry about. Guy Finch might have seen the person who'd killed his mother—nobody seemed to know how long he'd been in the house. The local police, damn them, didn't care; he'd been there, the murder had happened, and there you were, the rest was just tying up loose ends. Maybe FoFeality had had a hand in that decision, and maybe it was just incompetence; for the moment, no matter.

And Guy, any time I'd seen him, hadn't been in any kind of shape to be asked questions that had to do with the death; how long he'd been in the house, and who he might have seen coming or going, had to wait.

But—assuming he'd either seen somebody, or, just as simply, that it had been *possible* for him to have seen somebody—why hadn't the somebody, or a helpful associate, tried to kill *him*?

Of course, the somebody might be trusting to the inertia of the Columbus police force, which seemed to be considerable. And, whoever it was, he (or she) certainly knew that force better than I did. Even so . . .

It seemed neater to dispose of Guy Finch, if possible.

He was, of course, in police custody—but if Mirella could talk her way to the damn cell, somebody else could, too. Possibly somebody (like any Palace official—all our suspects, just for instance) with influence . . .

And the cell wasn't locked, or even effectively guarded. Guy was a sitting duck.

Maybe, I thought, somebody hadn't got around to that yet. Assuming our little Whoever was the same person who'd done the job on Astarte Finch (and there was one more reason than sheer timing to believe that—once again a mechanical had been involved, and our Whoever seemed to have a great fondness for mechanicals)—well, given that assumption, he'd been busy since the murder itself—arranging the Robbie warning for us, for one thing, and probably (it occurred to me) trying to get ready to do something about his duplicate Berringer.

That whole set of ideas made for muddy thinking—even if Guy Finch were at the bottom of the duplication process, he certainly wasn't at the bottom of the killing, or (therefore) of much else. But suppose somebody had hired him to do the duplicating job? The same somebody who had, further along, killed his mother?

That accounted very nicely for the degree of shock I'd seen. Guy would start feeling partly responsible for the murder, having been involved in shady doings with the killer beforehand.

And it made everything into one simple, neat picture. The only trouble was, I didn't believe it; Guy had been far too much the lovesick swain to be believable as the man who'd duplicated his light and love, and turned her off Guy Finch in the process.

Though he just might, I reflected, be *that* good an actor— "lovesick" is a lot easier to manage than "deeply shocked".

And, whether or not he was involved with the killer, he was certainly sitting on a target. I reached for the phone.

Mirella had gone to get the Totum, fed in basic specs and let it recognize Drone II and then, to my complete surprise, followed the Totum, and the dog it was now carrying off, to watch the Totum instruct Robbies, and (apparently) watch the Robbies feed and care for the dog

Or just possibly do the job herself. It seemed improbable, but still . . .

On the phone, I reached Meerande Fellm, and things turned upside-down again.

She had a businesslike way of answering the phone: "Fellm."

"Gerald Knave," I said. "I'm calling to ask about Guy Finch—if there's anything at all you know."

"I am close to the case," she said, "at my own request. As a Totum appears to be involved in some way, I have a certain expertise and interest."

"I understand the police think he's guilty," I said.

Meerande made a noise like a well-bred snort. "This is an opinion," she said. "It can be overcome. I admit there is weight behind it—"

"Weight?" I said, thinking of Horace FoF.

"Simply the weight of simplicity and convenience, I believe—though I am not certain," she said. "If you find one person alive at a crime scene, it is most convenient if that person is guilty of the crime. Such a conclusion means that much less investigative work need be done, of any sort."

"I thought the local police were better than that," I said.

"They deal with tourists, with small offenses," she said tiredly. "It is a well-funded force with little to do—Palace Security deals with most important cases, as they will usually involve the Palace in some way. When an event occurs which requires any complexity of treatment, they are almost without experience."

Well, that made sense. And Horace could still have a hand in things. "Wonderful," I said.

"But they are teachable," Meerande said, "if one is careful not to make it obvious that teaching is what is occurring. I think, in this case, Guy Finch will not come to trial. It will take time and effort—"

"Has he said anything?" I asked. "The obvious point—"

"How long was he in the house, and whom, if anyone, did he see there," she said. "I agree, of course. I have myself questioned him, but his responses have been—uncertain. His memory for the events remains very limited—which is, if I may be frank, a great surprise."

"My God," I said. "He's a kid, his mother has just been beaten to death—some shock might be expected."

"In a human, certainly," she said. "Shock of sufficient depth to erase much memory. But in Guy Finch—"

"Wait a minute," I said. "Isn't Guy human?"

"He is Mlang," Meerande said. "Adopted soon after birth—his parents having encountered a most unfortunate accident—and therefore an interesting study both for us and for humans. The adoption received much publicity at the time."

"Not in my orbit," I said. "I'm not on Earth all that much. But I can see that it would."

"Yes," she said. "My initial hypothesis now is that the human background he has had, through twenty-two years, has affected him emotionally—psychologically, one might say."

"And made him vulnerable to human degrees of shock," I said. My mind was putting pieces together rapidly. The oddly colored hair, and the yellow eyes. The concentration—the lecture-hall habit. I was faintly surprised I hadn't thought of the possibility before.

But somehow one never expects people to turn up as members of non-human races. If I'd been seeing Mlangs every week for ten years, Guy Finch as a Mlang would have been right there for me—but they're not a race I've had massive dealings with; as I've said, I'm not even sure whether or not I'd met any great number of them, before Meerande.

But it was obvious enough, once I'd been told. Well, most things are, damn it.

"Exactly," Meerande said. "Our comparative resistance to such shock may in fact be a cultural, not a genetic, artifact; but in this area little work has been done."

"It's fascinating," I said. "But let's clear the ground. There's no doubt the shock is real?"

"You think he may be disguising a role in the murder by assuming such a guise?" Meerande said. "No: there is no chance of it. It is real shock, with a real and unfortunate result."

"Has he got anything?" I said. "A glimmer, a fragment, anything to start from?"

"He remembers calling you," she said. "And he remembers someone—he cannot tell if the someone was his mother or her assailant—saying—screaming, rather—a few words."

"It's not much," I said, "but what were the words?"

Meerande cleared her throat. "*Stop*," she said. "*No more.*"

THIRTY-SEVEN

No, it wasn't much. And on analysis, it looked like even less.

It might easily have been screamed by a woman being beaten to death. It might just as easily have been screamed by the person doing the beating—who meant to stop her, to keep her from doing any more of something-or-other.

But it was what we had. I got off the phone after a little more conversation, and hunted up Mirella. She was in the kitchen, busily feeding the damn dog chunks of brown food, probably dog food found, bought or made by the mechs. There was a bowl for the food, but Mirella was doing the feeding by hand.

She looked up at me. "Dogs do better with people than with mechs," she said. "Everybody knows that." She sounded just the least bit defensive.

"You're probably right," I said. The dog gave a sound that was either a satisfied moan or a whine. Mirella dropped the bit of stuff she was holding back into the bowl, looked at Drone, and said:

"Okay, so now you know where the food is. Right here, come in any time." She got up and wiped her hands on a handy towel, and followed me into the living-room. I took a deep breath, sat down and told Mirella what I'd heard.

"Makes sense," she said. "I thought maybe his mother had had cosmetic surgery done on him—some places, it's a big thing, you want to look as not natural as you can imagine. Maybe here too; only nobody else has it. I thought, maybe she starts a new fashion with her kid—but a Mlang is simpler. Must have been a big, big story when it happened—Mlang kid raised by rich humans."

"But it's been twenty years and more," I said, "and things have calmed down. Now people talk about Astarte Finch and her son, and never turn a hair."

"Maybe a very small hair," Mirella said. "Claude Deke told you, away back the first time, not to judge the kid by the mother." She shook her head. "Not much of a hair," she said, "but now it makes more sense."

"So it does," I said. "And *stop—no more* isn't much either."

"You had to guess what people would say, somebody gets beat to a pulp like this," Mirella said, "that would be my second guess."

"What would the first be?" I said.

She shrugged. "Ouch."

All right, Guy wasn't human, he was a Mlang. How did this change anything?

I thought about the romance between Guy and Amy-Robsart. But humans and Mlangs (or so the story went) could even interbreed—and marriages, or liaisons or whatever it might be on Earth, had happened between members of different intelligent species. Sex life isn't the only reason for a marriage, and it isn't the only thing that keeps a marriage going, though if you judge by their books and their advertising, such of it as has survived, human Ancients, just preSpace, thought it was.

Sex is a very big extra—but it's an extra. Even the Ancients must have known that, or marriages involving (say) quadriplegics, the very elderly, and those otherwise incapable, wouldn't have happened at all—and they do seem to have happened, here and there. Very happily, too, as well as anybody can judge from this distance.

All right—there might have been a romance. But it might have been strained by the species difference—which gave Guy another small motive for creating a new Amy-Robsart who cooled off in a hurry. It still wasn't anything like enough reason to do the whole complicated job—but it put Guy an inch or so nearer to the center of things.

Regarding the murder, it made no change I could see. Guy hadn't done it—it was remotely possible he'd conked his mother forty or fifty times and then gone into shock, but it was the sort of one-in-a-million shot you didn't even worry about if you were charting possible collisions for Holly, the odd new planet-or-asteroid.

So somebody else had. That was logical, and neat, and not at all helpful. Mirella said suddenly:

"So FoFeality, why not?"

I stared at her. "For the murder? What were you doing, reading my mind?"

"Got to come out the same place," she said. "It's the only place there is. Guy's out, so maybe FoFeality is in? This would be very nice."

"The oily little weasel might have done almost anything in all this," I said. "A lot of it feels out of character for him—but he's made a career out of disguising his character, so what else is new? And he does know machines."

"So maybe Totums and Robbies," she said, "so maybe the shot at you and the poison at us, and also the warning. Which still does not make any sense."

"But he doesn't have a motive," I said, "unless he's involved in the Amy-Robsart switch somehow—and why would he be?"

Mirella shrugged. "Why would anybody be?" she said. "You change one Amy-Robsart for another, so you want her to do something. Now, it looks like, you want her to do something in Djakarta. But I think and I think, and I do not come up with anything worth the effort."

"She's an influence on her father," I said, and I knew what Mirella was going to say as soon as I heard myself come out with the same old reason. Knew it, and agreed with it.

"Influence she could be here," she said. "He is not making big decisions in Djakarta, he is being an Emperor. State visits, maybe he opens something. Shakes six thousand hands, smiles at everybody, spends a week and there you are, more votes for next time. Or not." She shook her head. "Big decisions wait for the Palace," she said. "So if Djakarta is a part of this, influence it can't be."

"All right," I said. "Then there's another motive."

Mirella gave me her fake sigh. "Think of one," she said. "It is easier to plant a bomb someplace, or a poison gas, or radiation that mixes up your head, or threatening letters. Not threatening letters to send the daughter to Djakarta, threatening letters to get something done, or not done. Whatever you want this Emperor to do, or maybe not to do, it is easier any other way. Building a whole new person—with changes, which still does not look possible—has to be harder."

"Not to mention building an entire new dog," I said. "But we're boarding one. I give it up."

THIRTY-EIGHT

"Only one little trouble with giving it up," Mirella said "So small I hate to mention, but still I have to."

"I know," I said.

"Amy-Robsart is still in two places at once," she said. "This is not possible, but it happens, and she is a good kid. And there is more."

"I know," I said.

"This little Whoever we have got trying to get at us, sending even warnings now—he is not going to give up. Or she. Or it, you want to cover all the bases, including the basest."

"I know," I said,

"And there is still a dead body," Mirella said. "So who made it dead? Not Guy." Her face brightened. "Me, I still like FoFeality for the whole thing."

"I agree with you about Amy-Robsart," I said. "A nice kid—what the Hell, somebody has to do something."

"And if somebody, then us," Mirella said.

"It all has to be connected somehow," I said. "Right. The bolt, the poison, the warning, the murder, the duplication—the damn dog with the warning, for God's sake—"

"Don't swear the dog," Mirella said. "It will give him bad dreams."

I shrugged. "Nothing like a canine nightmare," I agreed. "But look—it all has to be connected somehow."

""The dog connects," Mirella said. "A duplicate and a warning."

"I suppose so," I said. "I damn well refuse to believe a convenient twin dog. Guy said—away back—that some dogs couldn't be duplicated. So some can, and apparently Drone is one. Or he's been duplicated with changes—only you might have to watch them both together for a week to find out what changes."

"Right. Somebody duplicates a dog. Not a person, but still a new thing."

"Somebody," I said. "And we only have Guy's word for it that people can't be duplicated."

"Okay, but maybe it is a good word," Mirella said. "Who else would know?"

"Right," I said. "IGuy has to be involved. But he certrainly didn't commt the murder, and the murder is involved with everything else. And who dropped off the dog and the warning? Sten Rann, for God's sake?"

"I will not believe it," Mirella said.

"It's possible," I said. "Every damn name goes in the hat."

"It gets to be a big hat," Mirella said. "And who do we pick out of it?"

I said it once more. "I am damned if I know."

Back to the grind. And back to being targets, too—targets nobody, it seemed, was using.

We looked here and we looked there, we discussed and theorized and figured. A couple of long days passed—and, to our continuing surprise, nobody tried to kill either one of us.

In fact, nobody even issued us any more warnings.

"The natives," I said, "are quiet. Too quiet."

"So maybe thinking up new native stuff," Mirella said. But nothing happened.

And hour by hour and day by day, as the old song says, the date for Guy Finch's trial for the murder of his mother crept closer.

There were, of course, questions to ask—mostly of Meerande. The autopsy on Astarte's body told us that she'd been killed with the first or second blow, to the head—the other blows had followed, and there had been a lot of them, all fast enough so that some blood still flowed from the first few. That accounted, police were sure, for the splashes everywhere, and the blood on the Totum—their theory was that Guy had noticed the thing standing around—possibly having come in to hand Astarte the bottle she'd been found still clutching—and had just ordered it away, turned it off and done nothing more.

It explained why she'd still been clutching the bottle—she hadn't lived long enough to let go of it.

But it made no sense from any other angle—to begin with, it would certainly have been a Robbie who'd brought Astarte the drink; Totums were overseers, not direct servants, for most of the simpler purposes. And the turned-off Totum could hardly just have been neglected, except by a man in shock—but then, the police figured, Guy had gone into shock after the murder.

"It does happen, you know," Meerande told me.

"I know it does," I said. "And we both know it didn't."

She sighed, a sad little drone. "There is little I can do," she said.

"Look," I said. "Guy isn't human. Is he subject to human law? Isn't there some kind of diplomatic hassle you people could start?"

"Many years ago, perhaps," she said. "But the adoption was accepted then; its consequences—his subjection to normal human law in a normal human environment—must be accepted now."

For a couple of days, that suggestion was my main contribution to things. Then Claude Deke called me.

He wanted to know, of course, what was being done. I fobbed him off with a great many words, most of them polite, and, after hanging up, phoned the Palace myself. I got Sunny Samuels without much trouble.

"Amy-Robsart is very busy," she said at once.

I grinned at the phone. "But we set up an appointment," I said. "About the coffee."

There was the briefest of pauses. "So you did," she said. "For—"

"Two o'clock," I said. "Today. I'll be on time."

I was, too. Sunny wanted to stay for the presentation, which, she cautioned me, had to be very short—"Her busy schedule, you know," but I did manage to usher her out, telling her I'd only be a minute and using every ounce of charm I own, and most of my strength.

Drone I, thank God, was nowhere in sight. Amy-Robsart looked at me—seeming puzzled. I said: "We've got to talk," snd she nodded, just a little dreamily. Then her face seemed to come into focus.

"Guy," she said, and the one word was not only a sentence but a long paragraph.

"He'll be all right," I said.

"Who could have—who—" she started.

"Nobody knows," I said. "Nobody knows why, either. But it's connected to everything else, and there's a lot more."

She stared at me, open-mouthed. "That cannot be," she

said, and for that one second, and only for that second, she was Roesan I, Emperor of the Comity. I suppose she'd been around it long enough.

"It not only can be, it is," I said. "Take my word."

"But—"

"There is a connection," I said. "And I'll dig it out, and Guy will be all right."

"You know we wanted to go traveling—"

"To Haven IV," I said. "I know. To visit with the Tocks, and I'm sure they'll be delighted, some day or other. Whenever it is you're free to travel. I'll give you a note to Nassanank and Jessiss myself, and you can save it till then—not that the daughter of the Emperor—even when he isn't an Emperor any more—would need one—"

"Oh, please," she said. "And the—wait a minute."

THIRTY-NINE

What she wanted to do, as I'd hoped, was call off Sunny Samuels. The damn woman had been waiting outside—not eavesdropping, which, thank God, was impossible in a Berringer private apartment, but waiting anxiously for me to come out so she could go on . . .

Go on what? it occurred to me to ask myself. And when Amy-Robsart came back, I asked her: "Is Sunny always with you?"

""Well—usually," she said. "She helps out, you know. One must have someone, after all." She gave me a bright, cheerful smile.

"She wears a Security ring," I said.

Amy-Robsart frowned, puzzled again.

"Does she?" she asked. "I never noticed. I suppose she picked it up somewhere."

"Are they that easy to come by?" I said. "I'd think they'd be reserved, and if you weren't actually in Security yourself—"

Amy-Robsart shrugged casually. "Well, I really don't know," she said. "Somewhere around," she said. "Perhaps I ought to ask her."

"I wouldn't do that," I said.

Of course that conversation gave me about half the answer I needed—but I didn't know that then. We chatted for quite a while, Amy-Robsart and I, and she really was a nice kid—a little childish, perhaps, which is why people seemed to think of her as a girl, not a woman—but growing up under a spotlight can keep you childish a long time, because the people who aim the spotlight tend to protect you from all sorts of things, one of them called adulthood.

The dog never made an appearance, for which I was grateful; I am not a big fan of small dogs, and the one we had running around the apartment was going to fill my quota for several centuries.

I came home, in fact, to find the dog making friends—it did seem to want friends more than it wanted, say, prey—with a visitor. Claude Deke had turned up, and not alone.

His companion was, I admit, a surprise, though I suppose he shouldn't have been. We'd been discussing Horace, off and on, for so long, it was probably time he put in an appearance at the source of the talk.

Claude Deke was saying: "Good dog," in a patient voice, while the animal tried to climb up the leg of his jumper. Horace was standing a few feet away, looking very uncomfortable; well, I hadn't really thought he'd be the kind of person to make friends with pets of any description.

Mirella, holding the dog's bowl, which was full of brown chunks, waved at me with her free hand. "Claude here came to talk to you," she said, and the two men turned around.

Claude spoke first. "Knave, I really hate to do this."

I nodded, smiled politely in greeting, and went and sat down. The two men followed me. Mirella was watching Drone II, who had let go of Claude when he'd moved, and now trotted after him as if he'd been a plate of dog biscuits.

"Then don't do it," I said. "Problem solved. No fee."

"It's Holly," Claude said. I nodded again.

"Somehow I thought it would be," I said. I gestured at Horace. "But what's *he* doing here? My God, when we just wanted to chat, you were all over care and precautions, Colonization's little secrets—now what?"

"I asked him," Claude said, and Horace gave me a little smile. The smile said: *We're friends, everything has been forgotten, you'll do your nice friend Horace a little favor, won't you?* It was a lot for one thin smile to convey, especially on that round, sweaty little face, but he tried hard. Claude was going on: "It's a very important matter, Knave. And I've heard you and Mr. FoFeality were friends."

My eyebrows went up. "You heard that?" I said.

He shrugged. "You played billiards together," he said.

"Colonization, thy spies are everywhere," I said. "Semi-computer billiards, one game, and a week or more ago. Not exactly the basis for a lifelong attachment, Claude."

"Any influence he has on you," Claude said, "I want to use. This is important, Knave."

"Right," I said. "Tha last thing you said was important—"

"Well, that's not a problem now," he said Horace was looking at the two of us as if we'd been a tennis match. Mirella, having got Drone II's attention, was talking to it in a tone low enough not to disturb anybody, and I have no idea what she was saying. When I asked her later, she refused to tell me.

"Fine," I said. "And what do you want all this influence to do?"

"Holly," he said., "We need you, Knave."

"I thought Bruno Carr—"

"Carr's a good man," Claude lied. "But he's not—well, imaginative enough for a job like this. New questions to ask. New *sorts* of questions. He'll miss something."

"He sure will," I said. "Apparently he'll miss this assignment."

"Then you'll—"

"I will not," I said. "But you don't want Bruno. You'll find somebody else. Somebody perfectly fine for the job."

"I've found someone," he said. "You."

Mirella was sitting on the floor, near the damn dog, but the dog—who was now occupied with the food bowl—had lost interest for her. She was following the tennis game too.

"Not I," I said. "I'm on indefinite leave, remember?"

"Knave," Horace said, in as near to a silky voice as that hoarse little mutter could manage, "this is an important task. Important. You ought to think very carefully, very carefully indeed, before coming to a decision—"

"I thought carefully nine weeks ago," I said, "when I applied for leave, and got it. Holly is a fascinating place, and I look forward to finding out a lot about it in future—from somebody else's reports." I grinned at Claude Deke. "When, of course, they're made public."

"When I asked you to help out on another matter," Claude said, "you were willing."

"I was just barely damn willing, and it was only going to take a couple of days," I said. "This is going to take a year. No." I looked at them both. "And just whose idea was this to start with?" I said. "Yours, Claude? Or—just possibly—did Horace here come to you with the suggestion? I don't doubt he knew all about Holly long ago—Palace Security isn't good for much these days, God knows, but as a rumor-collecting device it must still be operating fairly well." Claude looked uncomfortable. I went right on: "It was Horace, wasn't it?" I said. "He suggested that, as Holly was such an unusual place, it needed your best man. And—"

"Well," Claude said defensively, "whoever suggested it, it is, and it does. And let's not beat around the bush, Knave: you're it."

"I may be it, but I'm not playing," I said. "I'm through with Surviving for a while, Claude. But I don't think I'm through with Horace."

"Mr. FoFeality simply made a suggestion—"

"Backed with everything he had," I said, "and coming along himself to add a little push, if possible. Horace—I've been calling you Horace; you don't mind, do you?"

"Not at all," the little weasel said. "Not in the least. We're friends; follow any script you like. Any script, as you please. Friends."

"Not quite that," I said, "but Horace will do, and thanks. You wanted me very completely out of the way—isolated for a year on a new planet, figuring my way out of whatever the Hell Holly decided to throw at me—far, far away from the Palace in Columbus, Ohio, NA, Earth." I stared at him. "Why?"

"You're the best man for the job," Horace said. "The very best."

"Yes," Claude said, and as he went on a light came on in my head at last. Although . . . "Because you don't follow a script—not the book, not any script. You follow your own head, and it's been a good one for us over the years."

"And you're deeply interested in Colonization, right, Horace?" I said. "After all, anybody from that little pill Cuchinar is a supporter of the big Comity colonization program—find enough promising new worlds, and Cuchinar may become entirely uninhabited."

"Knave—"

"Don't stand there and resent me," I said. "You need me—you need me going far, far away, as quickly as possile. I asked you why."

"And I told you," the little weasel said. "I just did that, I told you."

"Not good enough," I said. "I've been looking into Claude's little matter—let's not beat around the bush, you know all about it—and you want me not to look into it any more. I've had warnings—"

Claude said: "Warnings?"

"A Robbie, with a dog," I said. "There's the dog." I pointed at Drone II. "The Robbie's long gone. This whole situation has been lousy with mechanicals.'

"There are a lot of them on Earth," FoFeality said. "Quite a lot, counting all the very varied uses—well, a Survivor doesn't take them to new planets, of course, never does that, so you may not be familiar—"

"A Survivor lives a perfectly civilized life between assignments," I said. "Or when on indefinite leave, God damn it. And I have been living one—and you ought to know it, Horace. I own a Totum that gave you a small surprise last week."

"So you do," he said. "So you do indeed. Nevertheless, the fact that mechanicals, ordinary mechanicals, are involved—"

"Might mean nothing," I said. "The fact that you stand around looking suspicious may mean nothing too—and you do look suspicious, Horace; you can't help it, it's the result of a dedicated life. There's been a lot of talk about the least likely person—"

"I told you," Mirella said, but whether to me or to the dog or to the assembly she didn't make clear.

"But everyone looks for the least likely person these days," I said. "It's a fashion—and the least likely person is likely, given the fashion, to be the *most* likely person."

"Knave," Claude Deke said slowly, "what in Hell are you talking about?"

"Murder," I said. "Which is odd, because this whole plot didn't start out to be about murder. It started out to be about— well, influence, maybe. Maybe." That was the trouble; I had it all, and I didn't have a sensible motive. But I went on, because, damn it, I *did* have it all, didn't I? "And I think the plotter was a little startled by it, when it happened. Both times—but a lot more the second time."

FORTY

"Murder?" Claude said. "Astarte Finch. Twice?"

"A man named Glenn Hanford," I said "Nobody meant to kill him—he was a pure accident, in the wrong place when a Robbie's knee-bolt came by—but if you rig the bolt to shoot into a crowd, and it kills somebody, that's murder."

"Glenn Hanford?" Claude was having trouble keeping up, and no wonder.

I took a breath. "Claude, use the phone," I said. "Call the Columbus police department. Get a woman named Meerande Fellm—she's a Mlang, but never mind that. Tell her to get over here right away, in force—and tell her I've figured out what the odd smell was about."

He didn't move. A *lot* of trouble.

"Odd smell?" he said.

"Fax paper," I said. "Do it."

FoFeality was staring at me.

"You've gone mad," he said. "Entirely mad, Knave. You don't know what you're saying; you haven't the faintest idea—"

"A faint idea is what I did have," I said, "but it's cleared up nicely, thanks, and it's completely visible now. Mirella—"

And Mirella did as bright a single thing as I remember anybody doing. She stood up, looked down sternly at Drone II—who was, luckily, just backing away, full, from his food bowl—and said: "Watch him."

Drone II didn't do anything in particular; he stopped and looked at Mirella. She made it a big, sweeping gesture, pointing her whole arm at FoFeality—and the dog's head followed the gesture. She had to nudge him a little with her foot, but he turned to stare at Horace.

The little weasel stiffened, looked at the dog—and wilted. Well, he'd been very uncomfortable with Drone II from the first second I' d seen him, and Mirella had had the chance to see even more of the discomfort. The odds were he was afraid of the animal—and unfamiliar with what it could do.

He reacted just as if Drone II had been an immense slavering hound, summoned direct from Hell. He backed away, slowly, and when he found a chair behind him he collapsed into it.

Claude Deke was on the phone, saying something to some-body I hoped to God was Meerande Fellm. The rest was silence, for about a minute and a half.

Then FoFeality said: "I have a lot of influence, Knave. A *lot* of influence."

"Not any more," I said. You're done, Horace."

"The Emperor—"

"Is going to be fascinated by your attempt to fasten on to his daughter, like a parasite, and put her in danger."

He blinked. "What danger?" he said.

"My God," I said. "Guy Finch is in jail, accused of murder and—if your hopes bear fruit—about to be convicted of it. He and Amy-Robsart were in a plot together. Do you think she isn't going to try anything she can to blast that trial out of existence? Anything at all—whatever the publicity does to her, or to her father, or anybody else?"

"Publicity isn't fatal," he said. "Words, it's only words, Knave. After all—"

Drone II picked that moment to burp, or whine, or some-thing. FoFeality stiffened as if shot, and shut up.

"You shouldn't have come along, Horace," I said. "You re-ally shouldn't. It started me thinking—and once in a while, when I think, I arrive somewhere."

"It's all words," he said, looking at the dog.

"You've been behind everything," I said, and as I heard my-self say it, I knew it was wrong. Horace tore his attention from the dog for a minute.

"What do you mean, everything?" he said. "Everything—what do you mean by that?"

Claude Deke said: "You mean—everything that's been hap-pening—"

"A tourist was killed during the Changing of the Guard," I said. "Astarte Finch was murdered. There have been other events." The poisoned prawns, the Robbie with a threat . . . but my head was whirling. I knew I'd been wrong, as surely as I'd known I'd been right, and I didn't consider how Claude had to react.

"A threatening letter," he said. "That could be treated as tresasonous, you know." Horace turned to him, and the expres-sion on his face was honest surprise—or as near to honest anything as that face could get.

"He didn't," I said. "The note—"

"What threatening letter?" Horace said. "Treason? Why don't I know about this? Why doesn't Security—"

"I suppose people thought it better—" Claude began, not mildly—I'd convinced Claude, though I'd convinced him of the wrong thing. Horace gave one word an acid, hoarse turn:

"People?"

I took up the thread. "I told you to keep out of things," I said to Horace. I made it sound as strong as possible, and Drone II helped out again with a small yap, possibly one of sheer boredom. Horace cringed a little. Apparently any experience the man had had, of any kind of dog on the planet, was so far in his past it was only a vague mist. Even Drone II was a Savage Monster, as far as Horace FoFeality was concerned.

But he held on to most of his wits. "You talked to me about the murder of Astarte Finch," he said. "Not a threatening letter. Not treason. I should have been informed from the very start—"

Nobody, I told myself sadly, was that good an actor. Horace was sincere, damn it, and I'd been wrong.

I'd also been right, but I was going to have to sort all that out later, and with Mirella. She, being a bright person, hadn't said a word since pointing the dog at Horace.

I reflected that little Lily, the Palace maid, hadn't said a word either, and I made a silent and unnoticeable toast to her, and to Sten Rann, who must have used up all his persuasion to shut the young woman up.

But Mirella spoke up right then, interrupting Horace in mid-flight.

"You?" she said. "You should be informed? Of anything anywhere, you should be informed?"

Her voice was a bath of scorn. Horace looked at her, and his face became earnest. There were people that open, earnest look might have fooled, somewhere—there had to be.

"Madam," he said, "Ms. Puffer, Mrs. Knave, whoever you are—I am the head of Palace Security. As such—"

I am His Highness' dog at Kew. Pray tell me, Sir, whose dog are you? The lines went through my head again; they were exactly Horace's tone, high and superior.

Mirella had no Alexander Poop to slow her up. "You are the head," she said clearly, "of the worst police force I have ever heard about, anywhere. That is a lot of police forces, and there is no contest."

"Madam—" Horace said.

"I am not a Madam, I am a Mrs.," Mirella said. "You like it better, I am a Lance-Corporal of Police, for a real police force. Not this bunch of layoffs you have made out of maybe some good people and probably some good ideas."

"I run an effiicient service," Horace said icily. "Efficient. Words, it's all words."

"It is layoffs," Mirella said. "It is the Mars Brothers, and I am ashamed to be a police person when I see it."

She turned on her heel, and she left. Behind her, she left the longest silence I can remember.

Then Horace said: "I wonder why the woman is so angry."

For the first and last time, we were having the same thought at the same time.

FORTY-ONE

But I'd ask her later, and I was reasonably sure she'd make sense out of it. Meanwhile, there was the little problem of being right and wrong at the same time. Horace had said he'd had nothing to do with the damned threatening letter—which was to be expected. What was not to be expected was, I believed him.

But he was, obviously, involved with the mechanicals' end of things. His helping Claude Deke to get me out of sight—his having given Claude the idea in the first place—was the final nail in that particular coffin.

Well, we'd been saying all along there were two separate things going on, stitched together somehow into one thing. Why was it a surprise that Horace had been involved with one thing and not with the other?

Because, damn it, everything began with the duplication, didn't it? And the picture of Horace finding out somehow about the process (which sounded as improbable now as it had when Mirella and I had talked it over) and hiring Guy Finch to do the job on his light and love—well, Horace was a persuasive gent, if you were fool enough; but that, I told myself, would have to be the Hell of a massive job of persuasion. Horace didn't seem up to it; I doubted that the best hypnotist known, backed up with bombs, beamers and assorted mayhem, would have been up to it.

Which left me—where?

Well, there were all the mechanicals' tricks . . .

"Whatever she's angry about," I said, "she's not as angry as a few other people are going to be. Glenn Hanford's relatives, for instance—that's the name of the tourist who got killed during the Changing of the Guard, in case you've forgotten. And Guy Finch—his mother is dead, and a Totum was involved. In fact, a Totum committed the murder—in a way."

Horace made a remarkably unpleasant sound. If you were generous, you could call it a snort. "Totums can't commit murder," he said. "They simply can't, you know. The basic safeties—"

"A Totum can't harm anybody," I said. "Except by accident—I suppose one could fall on you, during a tornado or some such. And there have been a few damn fools who've killed themselves playing around with the wiring—though the Totum isn't at fault in either case."

"But Astarte Finch didn't die like that," Çlaude said.

"Perfectly true," I said "But part of a Totum can fall on you—several times. If suitably arranged."

Horace was looking smug and calm, and it was something of a strain. Claude said: "Knave, what in Hell are you talking about?"

"If you tell a Totum to detach its arm," I said, "what happens?"

He shrugged. "The Totum detaches its arm," he said.

"If you then use the arm as a club to beat somebody to death—" I started.

"But the Totum in the house wasn't in pieces," Horace said calmly. "Not at all, it was a single object, quite completely put together. Quite completely."

"True," I said. "And in order to reattach the arm you'd have to turn on the Totum, wouldn't you?"

"Of course you would," he said. "Of course. And the Totum, seeing a human being in need of aid, would react at once—at once, Knave. Basic safeties—"

"Which it takes time, care and an expert to sidestep," I said. "But they can be sidestepped—anything can, Horace, as I was saying about my own safeties a week ago."

"Your own—"

"Never mind," I said. "But you'd need to go about it step by step, and not make a slip. It's a complex process, Horace—it would have to be, safeties being what they are—so you wouldn't want to depend on your memory, if you could help it."

He said it, this time. "Knave, what are you talking about? This is just words, just—"

"A script," I said. "Claude here was saying, just a few minutes ago, that I didn't use one. And I don't. But you did, Horace. You had five sheets of fax paper—step-by-step instructions for the Totum, and for your own work. You got the Totum to hand you its arm, you turned it off, you used the arm—"

"In order to reattach the arm—" he began.

"The Totum would have to be turned on," I said. "But you could turn it on only partially—bypassing the recognition signal."

"It can't be done," he said. Not as calmly as before. "The basic safeties—"

"You can do a lot with recognition signals," I said. "You can even use them to locate another Totum, can't you, Horace? I should have seen that at the start, but I'm not a mechanician. You used them to locate my Totum, Horace—the one you abducted."

He bristled. "You said—"

"I said, if you stayed out of things, I'd keep quiet," I said. "And you didn't stay out—here you are, Horace—and the quiet time is over."

Claude Deke said: "I don't understand one word of this."

"You will," I said. I turned to Drone II, and said: "If that man makes a sound, he's yours," and pointed at Horace. A couple of seconds went by in silence.

"Well?" Claude said.

"Horace here," I said, "kidnapped my Totum recently, and gave it some new instructions. They didn't work—I've got safeties, too, Horace—but he did give it a good try. I have the whole thing on tape."

"He kidnapped—"

"My Totum," I said. "Never mind that now. It's Astarte Finch we're concerned with—and Glenn Hanford."

"And—"

"Not Amy-Robsart," I said. "Not yet." That was the other piece, and sooner or later it was going to make some sense.

But, as I'd just said, not yet.

"But on Astarte Finch," I said, "things are clear. That fax paper—"

"There was no fax paper," Horace said—and caught himself, and looked nervously at the dog. I gave Drone II a meaningless gesture, and Horace quieted down.

"You burned it later on, naturally," I said. "But it was there—your script to manage the Totum—and it confused the Hell out of us for a while. But—"

"Us?" Claude said.

"Later," I told him. "Look: Horace FoFeality clubbed Astarte Finch to death. Blow after blow, rained down on a bleeding, dying body."

"My God," Claude said. Horace had turned a faint but noticeable shade of green.

"And it got to you, didn't it?" I said "Conniving, suborning, all that is right in your line, isn't it, Horace? But actual death—Glenn Hanford was just a face in the crowd, and you never got close to him. An unfortunate accident. But you had to do the job on Astarte Finch all by yourself—up close and personalized, as they say—and you thought you could do it. It looks so easy on the 3V—one blast, one blow, it's all over, fade to black. No rage, just a thorough job of work. Making sure. You'd never done it before, and you couldn't take any chances at all." I looked at him. "But in person, it isn't quite so easy, is it?"

"Easy?" he said. It was a croak.

"That's why it was the last try," I said. "It got to you. You were sick—anxious, worried, sick. From then on—just the warning." I turned to Claude. "Not the threatening letter—this was something else. Another mechanicals' trick, and right up Horace's alley—nobody hurt, nothing but—as he keeps saying—words."

Horace had wilted. Claude cleared his throat. "But what *about* Amy-Rob—about Ms. Berringer?"

FORTY-TWO

It was a good question. It went on being a good question long after the Columbus police had arrived, and Horace had been taken away. Claude left soon after that, bemused, confused and only slightly cheered by my assurances that everything would be settled soon.

I needed some assurances of that myself. And I needed an answer to that question about being right and wrong. But I went to the kitchen, first, and asked an easier one.

Mirella only shrugged. "Nothing else to do," she said. "I will not say it was a pleasure, because it *was* a pleasure, and I should be a better person. But, pleasure or not, it had to be done."

I'd known, of course, that she hadn't stormed out in a fit of real anger. She'd have stuck around to see the fun and join in it, unless she'd had a very good motive to do otherwise. Apparently she'd had one.

"I'll bite," I said. "Why did it have to be done?"

She grinned at me. "For once you admit it," she said. "I was faster. I saw it happen, the dog was wearing out. Give it a little space, it would warm right up again for him, but it had to have the space."

I shrugged. "He looked just as scared of Drone II as ever," I said.

"Not if you look for small signs," she said. "You were busy figuring things—you got some puzzle still, and I know what it is—so that left me room to relax and look. Anybody sees better, she's relaxed. Or he."

I have no idea whether that's true or not—I seem to see best when everything's strung up to fever pitch—but I wasn't about to argue it. "So you provided a distraction," I said.

"Had to be loud, had to be sudden, had to not look like a distraction," she said. "Get him all busy about what I said, he would have time to rest up from the dog. To forget the dog is there, almost. Then it would be a threat again, when he looked again."

"Worked like a charm," I said. "Congratulations."

"All the same," she said, "there is one puzzle left. I have

been thinking about it."

"The duplicate Amy-Robsart," I said. "The puzzle we started with. Everything else has been cleared up, more or less."

"Not everything," she said. "The threatening letter is still there. But the threatening letter is the key."

"How?" I said.

She shook her head. "That," she said, "I don't know. Not right now." Then she grinned. "But it will come to me. In a dream, maybe. Or a word, somebody whispers in your ear and very sudden you know it all."

It wasn't a dream, and it wasn't a whisper. But it was, as it turned out, a word. Strictly speaking, two words.

We discussed the letter, and the duplication—and Guy Finch, of course. Guy would now be released with much regret, once Horace had been fitted for a cell—the police wouldn't like it, because Horace would have been friendly with altogether too many of them, but there was no way to duck a second of that.

Claude Deke, after all, swung a fair amount of weight himself—and Sten Rann would swing a lot more, with the Palace behind him. Horace had influence to spare, sell and trade to the natives, but all of it wasn't going to be enough to counter the combination of Palace influence and official—i.e. Bureaucractic—influence those two would be able to use.

And there'd be more—Meerande had to have friends on the force somewhere. Horace undoubtedly had his own friends there, sure—but he certainly hadn't managed to get every officer off in one of his confined little corners for a chat, and the ones still honest would count for something, too.

We discussed that—with some pleasure, whether or not the pleasure made us bad persons—and went back to the duplication and the damned letter.

And the words surfaced. They were: "not serious".

For once—well, maybe twice—Mirella was ahead of me. Well, it was her kind of thing, really, when you saw it all.

"Serious," she said, "is, first a note and then another note. Or a bomb or a riot, whatever. Serious is, anyhow, you mean it, you want it to happen, so you push a little. Serious is not one little note and then you shut up."

I looked at it. "Right," I said. "We had the note, and nothing else."

"So somebody wasn't serious," Mirella said.

"Damn it," I said, "we've had two deaths, we've had a couple of personal attempts, we've had a warning and a kidnapped Totum—"

"All of which was FoFeality," she said, "and let us celebrate when we get time, we have maybe made Security secure again. Not to mention even the local police people—must be some good ones there, besides this Mlang you talked to."

"Must be," I said, "and right again. But there is also the duplicated Amy-Robsart Berringer—which our Horace had nothing to do with."

"Nothing?" she said. "Maybe not much, but not nothing. When you see it all, it is very simple."

I nodded, tiredly. "It usually is," I said. "Lay it out for me."

She grinned. "No way," she said. "I am going to invite some people, and we are going to have a big thing here. I am a police person, and I know a lot of old detective stories too—some I knew before, some you showed me."

"And?"

"And for once I am going to be the big star in a detective story," she said. "We will get people all together, and I will say, here it is. I will even deduce a little."

I said it again. "And?"

"And you will know when everybody knows," she said. "For one time in my life I am going to be the star. Not a simple barefoot police person, not a Lance-Corporal—"

"Not a Mrs.," I said, and she grinned again.

"No, always a Mrs.," she said. "That we got, that we will have. But also a star. Wait and see." And she added: "I will give out one hint. Like all the stories, right?"

"One hint," I said. "All right: give."

"It is the least likely," Mirella said, and that was all she would say.

Of course, it was enough—after a little thought. It probaby is for you, too. But I wouldn't have spoiled Mirella's party for the world; she'd got there first, and she was entitled to the star role, the blue ribbon and anything else I had around or could find.

She invited Claude Deke and Sten Rann, and she invited Lily, the maid who had found the note. ("So why not give her something good she *can* talk about, maybe for weeks?") She invited Guy Finch, who was out of jail within days—as I've said, with regrets.

Not regrets expressed to Guy Finch, or regrets about his treatment. Regrets that the nice simple case, that needed next to no actual work, had been replaced by a large, hairy case that was going to require days and weeks of careful sifting—Horace's spiderwebbing being what it was—and then a very careful, absolutely strict and rigid, examination of the police force itself. They would come out of it a better force—but you couldn't expect them to be happy about that, not yet.

She invited Sunny Samuels, and she even invited Amy-Robsart herself. To my faint surprise, Amy-Robsart accepted—I supposed, Palace gossip being usually the fastest means of communication known, she'd heard about the guest list, and wanted to be in on things, however they were going to turn out.

She was going to be accompanied by somebody from Security, naturally—the whole drama was going to take place in our living-room, and we barely had enough chairs and little tables for the crowd (I hired in an extra Robbie, to ensure ease of service for everybody), and I was neither surprised nor especially pleased to find out it was going to be Godney Thrall, the man with the topee.

I worried—until I had the thing figured out for myself—that something was going to blow up before the party, but Mirella was calm. "Nothing will happen," she said. "Not serious is the key, and if there was going to be a something we would already have had it."

I took her word for it, a little uncomfortably, until I did have things figured out. After that, I was as calm as she'd been all along.

I am not much on actual gatherings in which the detective lays out all the clues and shows everybody how to fit them together into an answer. One of the members of such a gathering is likely to be the criminal you're after, and when the detective starts laying things out clearly he is likely to get shot, or otherwise damaged. This does not make sense—the gathering itself is more likely than not to catch the felon right then and there—but criminals seem to tend even more toward panic than the rest of us do. This time, though, Mirella was serenely sure there would be no danger ("FoFeality is out of the way, and with him gone why not things running smooth?"), and, when I'd followed the trail of reasoning to the same conclusion she'd reached, so was I.

"Serene" may be too strong a word, but "calm" will do.

And, on a nice sunny early evening in Columbus, Ohio, NA, Earth, Mirella greeted our guests, made sure everybody had enough of whatever it was they were taking from the flock of Robbies, and began.

FORTY-THREE

She actually said it—more or less.

"I suppose you're all wondering who called you."

That got the puzzled silence it deserved, but Mirella shrugged it off.

"Nervous," she said. "Look, there has been some trouble, and some of you know it and some of you have not got a clue." A little stir in the audience—and it was set up as an audience, with Mirella standing by her own chair and facing them, and me in a chair next to hers.

It was Claude Deke who bit. "What trouble?" Sunny Samuels, in what was loosely the second row, was looking as nervous as that smooth face could look. Amy-Robsart, seated up front with Godney Thrall, all nicely topeed, on her left, had an expression on her face I labeled Royal Audience Look: she was gently smiling, and hardly at all there.

Deke was away to her left in the third more-or-less row. Mirella peered over at him.

"You heard some of it the other day," she said. "Not enough to make sense for you, but some. Okay. Here it is: somebody has figured out a way to duplicate people. And make changes while doing it, so the new person is kind of edited."

Guy Finch (third row, to Deke's right) burst out with it. "That's impossible."

Mirella nodded. "I know," she said. "Very clear, you laid it all out for me. Some things can be duplicated. Here is one, for an instance." And she waved a hand. On cue, our Totum came in with Drone II in his arms.

Amy-Robsart said: "Drone! What are you doing—" and Mirella rode right over her.

"Not Drone," she said. "Anyhow not your Drone, who is probably curled up safe at home. This is a duplicate, and we got him because somebody delivered him to us."

"Somebody—"

"A body called Horace FoFeality," Mirella said, and *that* made a stir. Amy-Robsart started to stand up, and Godney Thrall was right there pulling her (respectfully) back down.

"FoFeality?" she said. "What could he—how could he

have—"

"Aha," Mirella said. "The stitching. Also the motive." Amy-Robsart frowned. Claude Deke said:

"Someone duplicated Ms. Berringer's dog? How could this be done?"

"Ask Guy Finch," Mirella said. "He did it. Maybe weeks ago, maybe months. I would bet months."

"It was a laboratory effect," Guy said. Not explaining, exactly, just filling in facts. "Amy—Ms. Berringer was assured there could be no harm to the original animnal—"

"He's fine," Amy-Robsart said, to everybody. "But how—"

"How could he do it, FoFeality?" Mirella said. "First ask, how could he find out, and that one is very easy. Something happens in the Palace, he is going to know about it." She grinned at Sten Rann and at Lily, who was sitting between Deke and Guy Finch looking like Patience on a monument. "Mostly," Mirella said. "Just pretty recent, there was an exception, and thank you, it turned out useful."

"But the dog—the duplicate—was in the laboratory—" Guy started.

"Probably," Mirella said. "Once. Now, no. This FoFeality, he is good at stuff like breaking and entering. You checked on the dog maybe every day?"

"Well—"

"So who would?" Mirella said. "The original is safe, the original is fine, so you get a lab type to feed the duplicate, maybe walk him a little, why check every day? A FoFeality could walk in and take him, and the lab person would report no dog, and the report would take maybe a week to get to you. Maybe longer, the way things have been with you—reports do not get into a jail so quick."

"But why would anyone—" A new voice: Sten Rann, sitting in the second row, center, next to Meerande Fellm. Meerande was paying a lot of attention, not to Mirella, but to Guy Finch: curious, I suppose, about a Mlang with human upbringing. But she seemed to keep enough of an ear open to track the explanation.

"To show us something," Mirella said. "To show, somebody is duplicating human beings, and making changes. Which—" With one hand she stopped Guy Finch from saying it, and said it herself—"we all heard can not be done."

"Well, it can't," Guy said. "The uncertainties involved—"

"Right," Mirella said. "Wherever there is people, there is a whole lot of uncertainties. Not to mention uncertainties with cats and maybe some dogs."

"Drone could be duplicated," Amy-Robsart put in.

"So he got duplicated, and sat in a lab," Mirella said, "maybe being lonely for some company, because a lab worker is not much. And he got stolen, and dropped right here, by a Robbie. And who told the Robbie, he should do all this? Horace FoFeality, it is not open for discussioon."

Guy said: "But—"

"So he wanted to tell us, duplicating is possible," Mirella said. "Wanted to make a nice scare. A lot can be got out of a nice scare, you handle things good enough—and he was already working on that. Since the whole thing started, he has been working on that. And when Jerry started to look at everything, he got scared himself."

Claude Deke said: "How do you know all this?"

"Deducing," Mirella said. "Because deducing is, you look at things, and only one answer makes sense, so you throw out the rest. Sherlock Holmes."

Meerande Fellm said: "He is studied by police academies."

"So how else do I know about him?" Mirella said. "Okay—so ask one little question. Why does this FoFeality want us to think duplication is possible? Because he wants a scare. Because in a scare he can make maybe even the Emperor do what he wants. From behind the throne he can run things. Motive."

"And he found out about it—" Sten Rann said, with restrained anger.

"The way he finds out anything," Mirella said. "What he did with Security is a sin and a shame, but a good spy group they still could be. And he had a Security person on the inside."

Sunny Samuels fidgeted. Just a little.

"The Security person was maybe a little careless," Mirella said. "But as careless as she *looked* to be, nobody could really be. Jerry said it—one little question and her whole story fell apart."

"Who was this Security officer?" Sten Rann asked. Tensely. "I'm supposed to be informed—"

"Sure," Mirella said. "So you figured, people would inform you. So you didn't look. She wears a Security ring, even. Go ahead, stand up, take a bow. You did a good job, if maybe you consider everything. Not perfect, but who can be perfect?"

There was a little silence. Then Sunny Samuels said, in a tiny voice: "Well, I do wear the ring. I shouldn't. But—well, it doesn't matter now. I was assigned to—to keep an eye on things, you see. To make sure everything was all right—to— but I don't know anything about all the rest of this. This business of a story, of—"

"Still, you are not bad," Mirella said. "You don't open it up, you wait for your boss to say go. But your boss is going to say go any minute now."

"Her boss?" Sten Rann said. "FoFeality? My God, he's not here. He's—well, I dislike to say it, but he's where he belongs."

"In a jail," Mirella said. "Anyhow, out of everybody's way, which is where he belongs, right. But who says FoFeality was Sunny Samuels' boss? He got to her and he assigned her. But most of the time—except maybe for passing on news, a little— like maybe the story of our little dog—"

She gave Drone II a look I will swear was fond. Sunny Samuels said:

"Well—" and shut up.

"So probably yes," Mirella said. "But her boss? Who is it she works for?"

There was another silence. Then Guy Finch said: "Well, really, it wasn't—"

"Wasn't serious," Mirella said. "That, I know. Not serious is the key thing. Sunny—I can call you Sunny?—put on an act and it was not a serious act. One little question and it all blew away. And it was meant to blow away. It was meant that we should deduce it, and get it wrong. Like the duplicating humans—we are supposed to figure out it happens, and it happened to Amy-Robsart Berringer."

"Meant to—cause suspicion, you mean," Guy said. Mirella nodded.

"And worry," she said. "While the Emperor is off in Djakarta, stories will get to him. He was right here, maybe he could not be fooled so easy. But he comes back, already he is worried, fooling him some more will be easy."

"Fooling him?" Sten Rann said. "Mrs. Knave, what is going on here?"

"Ask the boss," Mirella said. "The boss of Sunny Samuels, and the boss of the whole plot." She grinned. "Not serious," she said. "So who would expect such a nice young person to be serious?"

And she waved a hand at Amy-Robsart.

FORTY-FOUR

Sten Rann said: "You mean she came back? The duplicate—"

"Came back?" Mirella said. "She never went away. Her father, maybe it's tough to fool him. Her personal maid, maybe even tougher, but fooling is not needed there, because the personal maid is in on things. Her boy-friend, maybe toughest of all, but also the boy-friend is in on the whole story. So it was not too tough, not even for a young kid. A bright one, but still a kid."

Claude Deke broke the silence. "Duplicate?"

"Later," Mirella said, "everything will be nice and clear. For now, just this: all the worry about a duplicate person was not serious. Because persons can't be duplicated. We got told that, we got told good. Only the expert figured, we were not supposed to believe it."

Sten Rann spoke up. "You mean Amy—Ms. Berringer herself pretended to be—"

"A duplicate of herself," Mirella said. "Changed. Maybe kind of slow, kind of vague. This is hard to do? I could be slow, I could be vague, who would think I was pretending? The whole thing, it was one big pretend."

Amy-Robsart spoke up. "We never meant to hurt anyone," she said.

"Just worry a little," Mirella said. "I know. So relax: hurt anybody, you didn't. The hurting, that was somebody else. Somebody who found out what was going on, and decided, maybe he could use the whole story himself. He never bothered you with it, he just stitched all his plans into your not-serious."

"But why?" Sten Rann said blankly.

"Why? Simple," Mirella said. "He gets everybody worried, he knows something about the Emperor's daughter, maybe she does not want it known—he goes along, he makes it worse, and then maybe he comes to her—maybe tomorrow, only now it won't happen—and he says—do what I tell you, or I tell your father everything. For a young kid, this can be a big threat."

"But—" Sten Rann said.

"So she can influence him," she said. "That, she has for him, right? He finds out about the little harmless plot, he takes a ride on it himself, this little thing FoFeality, and he makes it not so harmless. He figures, he has got her right where he wants her. But there is a problem. There is two problems."

"Problems?" Amy-Robsart said. She wasn't looking vague any more, or slow either.

"We started looking," Mirella said. "Me and Jerry. And Jerry anyhow, people know he is pretty good at looking. So maybe we would find out, and blow everything nice and open. So get rid of us, okay? This, he tried—first at the Changing thing, then with our very own Totum. He misses, but he tries."

"He never came to see me," Amy-Robsart said.

Mirella nodded. "That was for tomorrow," she said. "But now not. But he talked to somebody else. He talked to Astarte Finch."

"He—he—" Guy said.

"He did that," Mirella said. "He killed your mother, Guy." She shook her head sadly. "She knew something," she said. "Not a lot, maybe, but about the duplication, about the dog, she had to know. Because her son told her. And she might tell somebody else. So he had to say stop, and he had to stop her. Only it was not what he thought." Another shake of the head. "Killing is not so simple and easy, like it looks on maybe the 3V," she said. "He did it, and it made him sick. But he did it. Because—his plot, that one was serious."

"And Ms. Berringer—" Sten Rann said.

"Is the same nice kid she was last month," Mirella said. "Not serious—but she tried hard. Even stopped seeing her boyfriend a lot, so it would look better. So nobody would make the connection, too. In the end, even one little letter she sent, just to make more nerves, just to push a little more."

And everybody started talking at once.

Me? I sat there. It was Mirella's show—I'd figured it out, too, but she'd got there first, and she could field all the questions. She'd answered all the serious ones herself—all but one. Claude Deke asked that one, when things got just a hair quieter.

"But why?" he said. "Why would she have done this at all?"

"Over and over we got told," Mirella said. "An influence she can be. But for a big thing, for breaking a rule—not a law, maybe, but a big rule, like a custom for years and years—she needed more than just influence. She needed maybe a little blackmail."

"Blackmail?"

"Let her travel off the planet," Mirella said, "or the original does not come back. It is a big rule, it needed a big story. So blackmail. Not serious, and still serious enough."

"Just to travel—"

"That, she wants to do," Mirella said. "And her boy-friend, he wants it too. Maybe he wants it more. Mlangs are big on travel."

Guy Finch stood up, and threaded his way over to Amy-Robsart. "We didn't mean any harm," he said flatly. "And it was all my idea. She didn't—"

"Not important, and who cares?" Mirella said. "I will bet, he knows you are so serious about it, you will travel. Or wait until he is out of his office. This will not be too long—though to young people I know it looks long."

"Travel," Guy said.

"Together," Mirella said. "Because a good trip, like a lot else we do, it is better if it happens not for one person but for two."

END NOTE

The lines quoted (for a wonder, correctly) by Knave in Chapter Two appear in *Girl Crazy!* by George and Ira Gershwin (recently adapted and revived as *Crazy for You*), and come from a song titled *Goldfarb, That's I'm*.

Further reports on Holly may, or may not, be forthcoming—I'll have to wait and see what Knave decides to tell me.

And once again, some people ought to be thanked, including Jeff Harris, and Spider Robinson, who is an encouraging sort.